I0637292

"What do you see, Myles whispered.

"Something better than a fantasy. A woman who wants me as much as I want her. A woman who needs to be touched as much as I need to touch her." His hands brushed her arms, her spine, her hips, and she felt herself surrendering to the pleasure of his caress.

"Do you want me to touch you?" Myles asked. She nodded her head.

"Then say it. Say 'Touch me, Myles.' Let me hear your voice so I know I'm not dreaming anymore."

She was surprised she could speak above the raucous beating of her heart. "Touch me, Myles. Touch me . . . everywhere."

"Am I making you ache, Faith? Tell me," he demanded, pulling her against his hard length.

"Yes," she said, feeling her body molding to his.

"Tell me how to make the hurt go away," he said, playing her body with merciless accuracy.

"Please, Myles, don't . . . make me beg."

"I want you to beg. I want you so far gone you're begging me not to stop. Not now, not ever. . . ."

WHAT ARE *LOVESWEPT* ROMANCES?

They are stories of true romance and touching emotion. We believe those two very important ingredients are constants in our highly sensual and very believable stories in the *LOVESWEPT* line. Our goal is to give you, the reader, stories of consistently high quality that may sometimes make you laugh, sometimes make you cry, but are always fresh and creative and contain many delightful surprises within their pages.

Most romance fans read an enormous number of books. Those they truly love, they keep. Others may be traded with friends and soon forgotten. We hope that each *LOVESWEPT* romance will be a treasure—a "keeper." We will always try to publish

LOVE STORIES YOU'LL NEVER FORGET
BY AUTHORS YOU'LL ALWAYS REMEMBER

The Editors

LOVESWEPT® • 496
Olivia Rupprecht
Behind Closed Doors

BANTAM BOOKS
NEW YORK • TORONTO • LONDON • SYDNEY • AUCKLAND

BEHIND CLOSED DOORS
A Bantam Book / September 1991

LOVESWEPT® and the wave device are registered
trademarks of Bantam Books, a division of
Bantam Doubleday Dell Publishing Group, Inc.
Registered in U.S. Patent
and Trademark Office and elsewhere.

All rights reserved.
Copyright © 1991 by Olivia Rupprecht.
Cover art copyright © 1991 by Kevin Johnson.
No part of this book may be reproduced or transmitted
in any form or by any means, electronic or mechanical,
including photocopying, recording, or by any
information storage and retrieval system, without
permission in writing from the publisher.
For information address: Bantam Books.

If you would be interested in receiving protective vinyl
covers for your Loveswept books, please write to this address
for information:

Loveswept
Bantam Books
P.O. Box 985
Hicksville, NY 11802

ISBN 0-553-44142-6

Published simultaneously in the United States and Canada

Bantam Books are published by Bantam Books, a division
of Bantam Doubleday Dell Publishing Group, Inc. Its trademark, consisting of the words "Bantam Books" and the
portrayal of a rooster, is Registered in U.S. Patent and
Trademark Office and in other countries. Marca Registrada.
Bantam Books, 666 Fifth Avenue, New York, New York
10103.

PRINTED IN THE UNITED STATES OF AMERICA

OPM   0 9 8 7 6 5 4 3 2 1

*BEHIND CLOSED DOORS is dedicated
with deepest gratitude and admiration to
Dr. Frank Deleon—a gifted surgeon
who made our own miracle possible.*

Behind Closed Doors

One

"Maybe we won't be sick today, baby," Faith Taylor whispered, smiling down at her belly. Sitting in her kitchen, sipping a cup of tea and nibbling on a cracker, Faith focused on sensations that were still new to her: the feeling of wonder that made her want to laugh and cry all at once; the tingling in her tender, rapidly swelling breasts; the heightening of her sense of smell.

She stared at the snow that wrapped the Colorado mountain in a shroud of winter white. Yet the baby inside her was a warm, sweet companion, a comforting contrast to the cold outside. How fitting it seemed that this new life had begun since another had ended, she thought. Her sister, Gloria, had passed away six weeks earlier, but the baby that had been growing within Faith for over three months still linked them together in a very real way. That she had selfishly kept her pregnancy a secret from the baby's father was something she refused to worry about then.

Suddenly the front-door buzzer shrilled several times in rapid succession, startling Faith. She quickly got to her feet and made her way through her home, sidestepping a drafting table with her graphic designs. Another table stood nearby with a mound of unformed sculpting clay. Beside it was a second mound she kept covered with a dropcloth for personal reasons.

She reached the front door in time to hear a fist bang twice on the other side, and immediately looked through the peephole.

It was a man, but his image was too distorted for her to identify.

"Who is it?" she demanded. An instinct to protect made her press a hand over her belly.

"It's me, Myles," a familiar voice answered. "Open the door, Faith. It's important."

"Myles," she whispered, feeling her stomach sink at the same time her heart rose to her throat.

She braced herself to face him. What in heaven's name could have brought him here? He couldn't possibly know about the baby, no more than he could know the secrets of her heart, of the hidden chamber he occupied there.

"Open up, Faith!"

She took a deep breath and flung the door open. "Myles," she said brightly, hoping her nervous smile passed for calm and the color she could feel bloom in her cheeks would go unnoticed. "What are you doing here? "Denver's an awfully long way from Detroit and your dream machines on wheels."

For a moment he just stood there saying nothing, his eyes locking with hers. There was the uneasiness she always felt between them, something that could never be explored. Then, unable to help herself, she let her gaze rove where her hands didn't dare.

His sun-streaked hair was longer than usual, and it suited him, but there were flecks of gray she hadn't seen at the funeral. His tan was fading, and his cheeks were ruddy from the brisk wind. He was leaner now, his cheeks more hollow. Her palms tingled with the forbidden impulse to stroke and soothe away his tension, which was evident by the way he clenched and unclenched his jaw.

That was the first giveaway. Something was very wrong. He looked seductively rumpled, as though he'd just crawled out of bed after one hellacious night. He wasn't clean shaven but sported two days' untrimmed growth. His open leather jacket revealed a wrinkled flannel shirt with a button missing just above the fly on his faded jeans.

Realizing where her gaze had strayed, Faith jerked her attention back to his eyes. Eyes that were expressive yet guarded. His gaze shimmied down her length, warming and chilling her all at once, before locking on her belly. Instinctively, before she could stop herself, she laid her palm protectively over her middle once more.

"I saw the papers, Faith. Not all, I'm sure, but enough to figure out what the hell's going on." He shivered suddenly. "Aren't you going to ask me in so we can discuss this?"

She stared at him, speechless. *He can't know,* she assured herself frantically, desperately attempting to remain calm. Faith could feel intensity emanating from him. Like the powerful engines of the sleek roadsters he designed, the energy purred, pulling her closer. And here she stood, facing him, more vulnerable than ever before.

He held her gaze in challenge until her own body began to shiver—as much from the shock of his confrontation as from the January wind whipping through the purple sweat suit she wore.

Without warning, before she could utter more than a surprised gasp, he pushed past her and kicked the door shut with the heel of his snow-covered boot. He uttered a short curse, then added something about her catching her death of pneumonia.

"First and foremost, how is your health?" he demanded rather than asked.

"M-my health?" she stammered while she swallowed hard against the knot of anxiety closing her throat. She had to think. Lie through her teeth if she had to, but come up with a convincing story. "My health is fine of course. Really, Myles, I don't have the slightest idea what you're talking about. Why didn't you just call and save yourself the trip? You came here for nothing."

"You're carrying my baby and I made this trip for nothing?" His short laugh was ragged with frayed nerves. "Listen, Faith, I've been up half the night and I'm still practically unhinged from what I stumbled on in Gloria's strongbox. I'm not in the mood for guessing games and I've already got a belly full of subterfuge. I want to hear it from you. Are you or are you not carrying *my* child?"

Gloria's strongbox! What were the papers doing in there? Hadn't she and Gloria agreed that Martin would keep them, just to be on the safe side? He could be trusted. After all, he wasn't just their attorney, he was their first cousin and had been as close as a brother to Gloria. How . . . ? Why . . . ? Wait, Myles hadn't said which papers he'd seen. Maybe she could convince him he'd jumped to the wrong conclusion.

"Of course I'm not carrying your baby, Myles," she ad-libbed, praying he didn't hear the waver in her voice. "How could that be possible? Gloria told me herself you refused the idea of a surrogate. And let's face it—what you're talking about does require a degree of cooperation on your part."

His brows, which had been knitted in concern, drew together in a terse frown. His lips went tight, and his nostrils flared in angry silence. When his eyes slitted, she forced herself not to squirm.

"Usually. But in this case it appears there was more than a little deceit involved." He pulled a piece of paper from his shirt pocket and held it up in front of her nose. "Take a look at this."

The paper was all too familiar. She recognized it as her agreement to offer the baby for adoption to her sister, since Gloria's ovarian cancer had rendered her sterile. She and Myles had contacted adoption agencies, only to be told that her failing health made them too much of a risk. Desperate for a child, she had then called Faith and outlined her daring plan.

Faith tried to snatch the paper from his hands,

but he held it out of her reach. "Where did you get this?" she demanded.

"I told you. I found it, along with some other eye-opening surprises, in Gloria's strongbox yesterday. One of which happens to be a medical bill all the way from Denver. It delineated the charges quite nicely: Intrauterine insemination for Faith Taylor with *private donor specimen.* I suppose I owe them a thank-you note for being so thorough with their records."

"That proves nothing!" she urgently insisted. "The donor could have been—"

"It's no use trying to lie." He thrust both hands through his hair in agitation. "They listed me as the donor and even took pains to confirm the date the specimen was frozen. I find it very odd that that date coincides with the day Gloria supposedly took one of my specimens to be tested at the clinic. Almost as odd as my having to hand over another one since, she said, the first arrived too late. For some strange reason I get the distinct feeling the first one was never delivered."

Faith opened her mouth to spout something, anything, that would cover up the all-too-obvious deception. No words came.

"I came here to make sure you and the baby were all right and to work out an arrangement. But you seem to have your own ideas about this pregnancy and they apparently don't include me." Myles folded the paper and tucked it back into his pocket. "I'll hang onto this nice little incriminating piece of evidence. Just in case things get nasty and we end up in court."

"Court?" She repeated in shock. "What do you mean, *court*?"

"*Court,* as in that's just as much my child as it is yours. *Court,* as in the reason I was so dead set against Gloria's surrogate idea was the possibility of our ending up in a legal battle over custody of the baby. *Court,* as in since she went behind my back and did it anyway, I have proof positive you agreed to give the baby up for adoption—to me and Gloria—and I plan to hold you to it. *Court,* Faith."

Faith shook her head in mute denial. Morning sickness rolled up her stomach with a vengeance. She staggered back several steps, thinking that none of this could be happening, and that surely she wasn't going to be sick.

But she was. She felt sick to her stomach and in her heart. The baby was hers now. Hers to carry and nurture and raise. After Gloria died, she knew she could never relinquish the child to Myles. She couldn't tell him the truth, and guilt over the deception would have made contact painful.

"Excuse me," she whispered. "I think I'm going to throw up." Faith covered her mouth with her hand and half ran, half wove her way to the bathroom, knocking over a vase in her haste.

The sound of shattering glass snapped Myles out of his bitter fury. He shook his head as though getting a grip on his emotional overload, and went after her.

He caught her by the arm.

"Please, Myles," she said weakly, "I don't want you to see me—"

She gagged and lurched for the toilet. Something that sounded like a sob brought him to his knees beside her. He brushed her wheat-colored hair away from her face, feeling its silkiness for the first time. She jerked, as if his touch were fire.

"Don't pull away from me, Faith," he said quietly, firmly. "I'm just trying to help."

"That's not what you—" She gagged once more, then groaned.

"Shhh," he whispered, stroking her hair. "Take it easy."

He went suddenly still and stared at his hand. *What are you doing to her hair?* he asked himself in disbelief. He'd actually been playing with it between his fingers.

He found it amazingly difficult to pull back his hand. Myles snorted in self-disgust and hoisted himself upright. He caught a glimpse of his face in the bathroom mirror and saw raw need etched in the tautness of his features.

"Where do you keep the washcloths?" he said shortly.

Faith pointed an unsteady finger in the direction of a cabinet. Myles found a washcloth and wet it, feeling bad about his abrupt tone. He'd shaken her up enough with his threats. He hadn't meant to lose control and verbally attack her. That could only defeat his purpose in coming here.

He leaned down and pressed the cold cloth to her temples.

"Thank you," she whispered, and glanced up.

Faith had beautiful, stormy-gray eyes, he

thought, framed by sooty lashes that were spiked with tears he knew he was responsible for.

"You don't owe me any thanks," he said gruffly, and looked away. Then he looked back, unable to deny himself something that felt so good when for so long all he'd had was sorrow. "But I do owe you an apology, Faith. I'm not proud of how I behaved in there, barging in the way I did and bullying you around. You don't need that. Especially in your condition. Forgive me?"

She nodded, then smiled tiredly. Myles noticed for the first time how exhausted she appeared, like a rag doll put through a wringer. He'd heard that pregnant women could sleep ten hours and still crave more. Had Faith been getting enough sleep? Was she eating properly? And the baby—*his* baby—was he . . . or could it be a she . . . was the baby well?

Myles's gaze automatically fixed on her belly, and he felt the stirrings of . . . excitement. Pride. Something good that made him glad to be alive for the first time in ages.

Realizing he was staring, he lifted his gaze only to collide with Faith's. He felt off balance, like the time he fell out of a tree and knocked the breath from his chest.

She touched her hair in an awkward, flustered way, and he couldn't keep himself from remembering how vibrant and soft it had felt as it had spilled through his—

He squelched the thought before he could complete it and cleared his throat, trying to rid himself of the thickness that affected his breathing—and apparently his rational thinking as well.

Impatient with himself, he said, "Better now?"

"Better. It usually comes and goes until about noon."

Myles gave a curt nod and extended his hand. She took it, and while he helped Faith to her feet, he could feel his confusion grow in direct proportion to the sensation the contact elicited.

"I'll go clean up the glass from the vase," he said. "Then I'll put on some coffee and we can talk in the kitchen."

He noticed Faith's hands were shaking as she fumbled with the toothpaste. "I'd prefer the living room, Myles. The smell of coffee doesn't agree with me lately."

"Then we'll forget about the coffee. How about breakfast? Can I make you some eggs and bacon?"

Her complexion went from pallid to green. "No, really, that's all right. I've already had tea and crackers."

"Tea and crackers? What kind of breakfast is that? For heaven's sake, Faith, you're supposed to be eating for two, and that's not half enough for one."

"I'll eat extra tonight. I promise."

"I'll hold you to that."

Myles turned on his heel and strode away, putting much-needed distance between them.

He needed to clear his head and purge his thoughts.

He needed to get food down Faith that she wouldn't throw up.

Most importantly he needed to figure out how in hell he was going to clean up this mess the two women had pulled off behind his back, and keep the baby.

He'd lost everything else. He wasn't about to give up his only child.

Two

"Why did you do it, Faith?"

She stopped in mid-sip of the warm milk Myles had insisted she drink and studied the creamy liquid as she swirled it uneasily in her cup.

"You mean why did I agree to the artificial insemination?" she asked, unable to bring herself to look directly at him. He was studying her; she could feel it. He said nothing, and she went on, trying to fill the awkward gap with something impersonal when nothing could be more personal to both.

"You know, they don't call it that too often anymore. It's called intrauterine insemination. Those doctors are ones for abbreviations, aren't they? IUD, D and C, EKG, or in this case, IUI. It's really remarkable. There's about an eighty-five-percent chance of success, what with tests to monitor fertility cycles and—"

"Drop the terminology and level with me, Faith.

You made a promise, a very serious promise to a sick woman. It's not like you to take your word back anymore than I can imagine you being willing to give up your own child. I just want to know why you did it, before we consider our options. This is something that affects us both too deeply to be flippant about."

He caught her wrist, stilling her motions.

Faith prayed he wouldn't feel her pulse leap in response to the innocent contact and silently cursed herself for being a traitor to her sister, barely cold in the ground. Had Gloria ever guessed? Could she have possibly known what torture it was to stand up as the maid of honor and wish them every happiness at the same time that she, Faith, repeated the wedding vows in silence, so desperately wishing they were hers to make?

"You're right, Myles," she slowly agreed, thrilling to his touch when she knew she should be pulling back. "I do take my vows . . . my promises . . . seriously. Especially something of this magnitude. But it's complicated. Nothing turned out to be exactly perfect. Too many things went wrong."

His grip tightened momentarily before he took the cup and set it aside. She wanted him to touch her again, wrong or not, because she had loved him too long, she was too alone and all too human. She wanted him to touch her the way he had when he'd stroked her hair. She knew he'd only meant to comfort her, but the effect on her was anything but soothing.

"Look at me, Faith," he said in a low voice. When she hesitated, he did touch her again, tilting her chin up. A single tear of joy and sorrow and distress slid down her cheek. Then she felt the sensitive brush of his fingertip, callused from manual work, as he wiped the plump, wet drop. In that moment Faith knew she had been wise over the years to avoid even the most casual embrace of greeting, the most innocent kiss of good-bye.

"Look at me," he said again.

She did look at him then. As usual, she felt a tingling shock, as though a live wire had hit an exposed nerve.

Myles's hand tensed, and it seemed to jerk as he moved it away. His face took on a strained expression before he frowned and erased what she thought she'd seen.

"Why did I do it?" she whispered with jagged breath. "Because I loved my sister enough to do anything for her. Because the doctor said her will to live and her attitude were vital to recovery . . . and I thought it might make the difference. I couldn't live with myself if I thought there was one thing I could have done to turn the tide and held it back. Because—"

Because I wanted to make it up to her for falling in love with you before I had any idea she'd fallen in love with the same man. Because, Myles, I wanted to have your baby, no matter how it was conceived. . . . Because, God forgive me, I was human enough to want to give you something no one else could, not even your wife.

Faith took a deep breath. "Because I'm nearly thirty years old and I have no man in the foreseeable future and I thought it might be my one chance to have a child. I knew you and Gloria would be wonderful parents, and since I planned to move close by, I thought it would be perfect. You'd have all the responsibility and I could spoil the kid rotten without giving up my career." She gave a false laugh. "I'm a practical, modern woman. It made perfect sense at the time."

His expression hardened, and she knew with regret that she'd succeeded in convincing him of the lie.

"Well, it's nice to know that even with that kind of modern thinking you could make a decision that was humane. As for me . . ." He shrugged and pursed his lips in thought. "No, I don't think I could have been that . . . objective in my reasoning."

And Gloria would never have considered such a cold, calculating angle.

He didn't say it out loud, but she could hear the thought as if he'd shouted it, and it hurt. Deeply. She'd concocted the lie to disguise her real reasons, but why did he have to swallow it without hesitation? Now she felt compelled to defend herself.

"I had no way of knowing how attached I'd become to the baby. And it's not as though I wanted to put in only occasional appearances on birthdays and holidays. Gloria understood I wanted to play an important role in my child's upbringing and that's why I'd planned to move back. Between the two of us, the child would have the best of both worlds. She was so nurturing and competent, and I'm so . . ."

So . . . what? she wondered. Would she make a good mother? It was The Question that wouldn't go away. She wanted to be the best, but she couldn't be Gloria. Gloria who cooked and sewed and took every child she ever met into her arms. Gloria the steady one, the nurturer, the listening ear who always gave good counsel.

And what of her? Had the years really matured her enough to handle this? Faith could feel her bottom lip begin to quiver. What was wrong with her anyway? She never used to cry. But now the tears came when she read baby announcements at card shops, when commercials for long-distance telephone calls came on, when she heard sentimental songs. What had happened to the self-assured woman she had been? Now she felt so . . . so overwhelmed by it all. She couldn't cook, she couldn't sew. No child could want her for a mother.

An unexpected sob lodged in her throat.

"You're the kind of mother who would let your child have the time of his life while you helped him dig a hole in the ground to China." Myles leaned forward and took her hand. "You'd let him get filthy when he played because dirt washes off and having fun's more important than keeping a rip out of his pants. You might not make cookie dough, but you'd always be game to see who could make a jaw breaker last longest, or have gum balls handy for a bubble-blowing contest. You'd always know the top forty songs and be really 'cool'—for a mom that is."

She sniffled, and looked up from their clasped hands with a grateful smile.

"Thank you, Myles. You'll make a . . ."

"Good father?" he filled in when she trailed off.

He held her gaze with an unwavering, purposeful one of his own. Faith could feel the prickle of chills at the nape of her neck at the same time that her hands grew clammy and damp. Hormones, no doubt.

"What are we going to do, Myles? You know the truth now." Or most of it, she thought. "You also know I wasn't going to let you in on the secret. No more than I planned to give the baby up once . . ."

Gloria died. Oh, Lord, for once she wished they could talk without her ghost between them.

"You were going to go through with this all alone, weren't you? If I hadn't found those papers, you never would have told me."

"I thought telling you would make things more complicated than they already were. After all, we did deceive you. I had no way of knowing how you'd react. Whether you'd be angry or accepting or—"

"You were afraid that I'd try to take the baby away, weren't you?"

She nodded. "You threatened as much."

"I know, and I wish I could take it back. But you were denying it all, and I was angry. Desperate. You have to understand something, Faith. I lost too much." His grip tightened, and she returned the increased pressure. "My grief, it was like this living, breathing thing. It's been eating me alive, like a kind of . . ."

Cancer. The word hung suspended. Unspoken yet understood.

"I've felt it, too, Myles." She glanced at her belly and wished fervently that he could share her joy over the baby and the comfort she drew from it that made her own loss more bearable. If only the situation were different with her and Myles; if only she could lay his hand upon her belly and let him share the bond.

Instead she said, "I was only thinking of myself. Forgive me for that."

"What's done is done," he said. "What matters now is how we choose to handle the situation. I'm not going to try to take the baby away from you, Faith. But I'm not willing to bow out either."

"I don't expect you to."

"Then you do admit that I have a valid claim on this child?"

"You have the evidence." She flushed at the memory of her blatant denial; she didn't blame Myles for lashing out at her the way he had. The whole nightmarish scene was her fault too. "No, Myles. I'm not going to try to deny that you have a very real stake in all this."

"Good. But we're still left with big problems." He picked up the mug and handed it to her. "Drink your milk, Faith."

She obliged him, knowing it was for the good of the baby, though it certainly wasn't to her personal liking. Once she had a mouthful, Myles fixed her with a meaningful stare.

"I'll call a mover tomorrow to see about getting your things shipped to Detroit."

Faith choked on the liquid. Myles was immediately out of his chair.

"Faith, are you all right?" He began to pat her back furiously, his voice anxious.

She coughed hard several times, then caught her breath.

His face was mere inches from hers. The concern etched in his features shifted to something that was unmistakably male. His eyes met hers and darkened before his gaze lowered to her lips.

Myles could feel the shallow wisp of her breath fan sweetly against his skin. How long had it been since he'd felt this way? Felt the stirrings of his body, the urge to press soft woman-skin to his chest, his loins, to take it and caress it with his hands? So long, oh Lord, so very long. For so long he'd been surrounded by sickness until he thought it had invaded his own body as well.

And here was health, here was life, here was a woman he wanted with a sudden, staggering urgency. He didn't understand it. He couldn't accept it. But there it was, pressing in on him, urging surrender to the weakness of his flesh. A sensation of shutters snapping open gripped him, and he tilted her head up seeing her in a different light.

He stared at a face that looked back at him with confusion. She wasn't the young girl he'd worked with years ago. Flash had been traded in for quiet elegance. Gone were the trendy hairstyles, replaced by something simple but chic. The clothes in her closet were probably classic yet eclectic rather than funky.

In a discreet way he'd noticed her evolution. Only there was nothing discreet about what he was feeling now. His body leaned closer . . . closer. . . . Did she have to smell so good? Like the first whisper of spring after a harsh, lonely, endless winter.

He had to move away, get some space between them, or he would kiss her. Too much remained unresolved and his conscience was screaming obscenities at his libido for even thinking it.

Her tongue flicked over her bottom lip. Pink. Delicate. Satiny.

Sexy.

Myles forced his feet to move back and could only pray she didn't hear the groan catch in his throat. She would surely be insulted if she could read his thoughts . . . or worse, she would pity him, find his starvation of the senses pathetic.

A pity kiss. He hadn't stooped that low.

"Detroit?" she said unevenly, breaking the strained silence. "You mean you still expect me to move there, even after . . . And my lease here—"

"Can be sublet, and if not, I'll pay any penalty fees. It's the least I can do." Myles paced the room restlessly, needing an outlet of release. "Besides, you said yourself you'd planned to move before everything got so crazy. Why change your mind now?"

He was pushing her and he knew it, but damn . . . first the baby, and now this. This hurting pulse between his legs. This distress and impatience with himself for not having more control.

"But where will I live? I couldn't possibly—"

"Move in with me? Why not? It's a huge house.

We wouldn't even have to cross paths. Except at mealtimes." He managed a slight smile. "Just so I can be sure you're eating right."

What are you, nuts? his rational mind challenged. *You could share the Taj Mahal and it would still be too close for comfort.*

"Myles, I don't know if that's such a good idea. I mean . . . it's such an awkward situation. I need my own place. And I have to have a studio."

"You work from your home now as it is. Couldn't you keep your accounts just as well from Detroit? I don't think many of those advertisers are going to want to give up their best free-lance designer."

"You're flattering me now."

"But not falsely." He took a steadying breath. "Would you lose any accounts?"

"Maybe one or two, not many."

"I'll make up for any that you lose. In fact my company could use your talents. But the point is this. You can move your career. I can't. CEOs can't pack up and tell the employees to keep in touch."

"I . . . realize that."

"Then you also realize that it's impossible for me to be there for you and the baby unless we close the distance. Detroit's too far from Denver."

"I can't argue that. But—" She seemed to struggle with something inside herself before closing her eyes and saying hesitantly, "I suppose . . . perhaps if I could find my own place there. One big enough for a studio . . . and a nursery."

He couldn't believe his ears. Whatever her reasons, she'd given in much faster than he'd dared hope. Faith shifted in her chair, and he could discern the slight roundness of her usually reed-slim body. Pregnancy definitely agreed with her, he realized. Not only was she filling out, she had more color in her face. He liked seeing her cheeks so rosy.

"A nice place can be hard to find on a moment's notice. And as far as a nursery goes, I want my child to have the best. Don't you?"

"Of course. But, Myles, we can't live together, not even temporarily. I couldn't possibly stay in your house."

"Why not? Because it wouldn't be appropriate? Or because you're afraid this is just a ploy to get you under my roof so that after the baby's born I won't let you take it away?"

For a full minute she regarded him keenly. Then she shook her head. "No, I don't think you'd do that. Not as long as you could spend as much time as you wanted with him . . . or her."

He felt a smile slowly appear on his lips. It had been so long, the expression felt odd. And good, so good. He hadn't had time to consider things like nurseries and genders and spending time with a baby. *His* baby! He was going to have a baby! After all this time it was finally happening. Not as he'd envisioned it when he and Gloria had bought the big old house years before. They'd been careful and patient, at his insistence, waiting for his daring business venture to stabilize before trying to have children.

Then they learned it was never meant to be. Such a loss for them both. For the woman who loved even her preschoolers with a maternal passion. For the man who needed the kind of family unity he'd missed growing up alone with his hard-drinking, hard-living father.

Myles shoved his hands into his pockets and considered their options. At least he'd gotten her to agree to move to Detroit—his first purpose in coming here. The other major concern had to do with legitimacy and that was far more of a personal issue than a legal one. He'd have to work on that, and it would be a helluva lot easier to convince Faith if their proximity led to trust.

"Okay," he said, figuring he could convince her otherwise with time. "Maybe you're right. But for the time being you can stay with me until we find you a nice place. I'll even help, how's that?"

Slowly she nodded her head in agreement. Myles smiled grimly to himself. Amazing how he'd gotten his way and managed to rationalize his motivations all in one swoop. He'd just lied to Faith and almost succeeded in lying to himself.

He'd known what he ultimately wanted in coming here—to claim his baby—but didn't have a clue of how to go about it. He had a plan of sorts now, and that felt mighty good.

Only he was leaving with more than he'd bargained for: a conscience that was already robbing his pleasure in getting her to agree. And an ache in his groin he had no business feeling.

Just looking at her now, watching the way she unconsciously stroked her belly, he could feel himself begin to harden.

"Could you eat some soup?" he threw over his shoulder as he quickly headed for the kitchen. "It's time for supper, and you hardly ate a bite at lunch."

"Soup sounds good," she confirmed. "And there's some caviar in the fridge. I'd love some of that with a slice of pizza. After I get past the queasy stage in the mornings, I'm usually starved."

"Caviar and pizza." Myles chuckled. "Sounds . . . interesting."

"Ever the diplomat, aren't you, Myles? I know it sounds gross. But lately I get cravings for the strangest things." Her smile was a little shy. "Of course I'll have to change my eating habits once I start nursing the baby."

An image of Faith's unbound breasts sabotaged the small bit of control he'd mastered en route to the kitchen.

Quickly turning his back, Myles prayed for mercy. This was probably his punishment for feeling such illicit longing.

You've really done it now, hot shot. So what're you gonna do once she moves in?

"I don't know," he muttered to himself as he pulled out a frozen pizza and began to hunt for the caviar. "Heaven help me, but I just don't know."

Three

"First things first," Faith muttered to herself as she looked around the rooms she had temporarily claimed on the second floor. Her gaze lifted to the high ceilings tinted a delicate peach, then shifted to the big bay window, where a built-in seat and vintage needlepointed cushions beckoned her to rest her feet. She couldn't. Not when the Persian rugs on the oak floor were littered with boxes on top of boxes.

The duty call to Cousin Martin would simply have to wait. Though if she were honest with herself, she'd have to admit it was a call she wanted to put off.

"The movers are ready to leave, Faith. You're sure you don't want them to unpack for you?"

"I'm sure, Myles," she called out. "My friend Jennifer assured me it was easier to do it yourself and put things where you want them as you go along." She wouldn't mention there were certain things she wanted out of sight and that by un-packing herself she could keep it that way.

"Whatever you say. I'll see them out the door and be right back."

For a moment she stood there still disbelieving what she'd agreed to. Here she was under Myles's roof, albeit temporarily, filled with a sense of nig-gling guilt for her less-than-noble reasons. She didn't want to go through this pregnancy alone and she'd had plans to move her business to Detroit before fate intervened. That's what she'd told herself. But it was far from the real reason she was here.

Quite simply she was in love with Myles and she wanted to be with him, to . . . She closed her eyes. *Go ahead and admit it,* her mind chal-lenged. *You want a lot more than that. You want him to see you as a woman, a desirable woman who just happens to be pregnant with his baby. You want to be his lover and you want more than an affair. This is the once-in-a-lifetime chance you thought would never come.*

"They're gone. Now it's just you and me and the boxes. Oh, and the baby too." He chuckled.

She jumped at the sound of his voice close behind her, breaking into her self-examination.

"I can't believe I didn't lose any accounts," she babbled, saying the first thing she could think of. "Or that Jennifer pounced on the chance to sublet my place."

"I'm not surprised. As she said, she'd always envied your house." He moved closer until she had to look up to meet his eyes. "I do have to admit that

I'm disappointed over your not losing any accounts."

"Disappointed? But why?" And why did he have to stand so close? So close she had only to inhale to breathe in the male scent of him. He smelled of a subtle spice aftershave mingled with the light sweat of exertion.

"Why? Because I wanted an excuse to have you work with me—" He broke off and cleared his throat. "My company, I mean."

She laughed. "Your new line of roadsters speak for themselves, Myles. The critics are raving over your show cars. I don't think you'll see a slump without me."

"Hmmm. Well, after seven years in the making they don't seem so new anymore, and I still have my detractors, not to mention a lot of people who're still waiting for a return on their investment. But I suppose we'll have to limp along with the artists we've contracted." He touched her arm lightly. She shivered and he immediately withdrew. "I don't want to see you pushing yourself too hard. You need your rest and plenty to eat."

"Plenty to eat! Myles, you're fattening me up with all your cooking as it is. I'm even afraid to look at the scale. I've probably gained ten pounds since you banged on my door two weeks ago."

"If you've gained ten pounds, Faith, they went to all the right—" He stopped, his attention lowering to her breasts and lingering there. Suddenly he moved away and focused on a nearby carton. "Let's get started. We've got enough here to keep us busy until you go into labor."

She stood there, rooted to the spot. Her breasts still tingled from his gaze, as if he'd touched her without touching her. And what was this alien feeling of . . . resentment? She loved this baby with a fierce intensity. So why did it bother her that her conversations with Myles always led to the unborn child that had brought her here to begin with?

Before she could examine the disconcerting emotions she didn't understand, Myles began to unpack an object that was all too familiar to her. A very incriminating object.

"Don't touch that!" Faith lurched and nearly lost her balance as she made a grab for the covered sculpture.

He stopped in mid-motion, startled by her outburst, and spun around to break her fall.

"For heaven's sake, Faith," he grumbled when he grasped her arms. "You practically gave me heart failure." With a curt nod at the box he added, "What's in there that's so untouchable, anyway?"

"It's . . . personal," she said breathlessly. Faith was unsure whether it was from the close call or the nearness of Myles. He hadn't released her arms, even though both her feet were planted safely on the ground.

"Personal?" He raised a brow while his hands slightly tightened. "Now I'm curious. What kind of sculpture would be personal? I guess no one would be exactly sure what it was except you, right?"

She gave a slight nod, not wanting to encourage a guessing game and yet not wanting to end the conversation. His palms were warm through the fabric of her blouse, and his chest was all but touching hers. She could reach up and stroke his lightly whiskered face; she could pull his head down and taste his lips.

She would make an utter fool of herself if she did either. So she simply kept still so that he wouldn't move away, thrilling to his nearness, the underlying strength of his physique. The even stronger lure of what lay beneath: character, intelligence, maturity.

"And I don't suppose it would be animal, vegetable, or mineral. Even Lassie would have a hard time inspiring such loyalty."

"It's not important, Myles. It's just something of mine that I'm . . . attached to."

"Or some*one*?" His teasing smile gave way to an assessing expression as he studied her face for a reaction. When she shook her head in quick denial, Myles murmured, "Who was he, Faith?"

"No one," she said, feeling her apprehension rise with his accuracy. "No one important."

"But it's personal," he reminded her. "And frankly, I can't help but wonder about your personal life. Why you never married or talked about having a man in your life. You aren't exactly what anyone would call plain or dull."

"No, just a little skinny and weird. Typical artist." She laughed shakily, glad to get off the subject of the sculpture but not exactly thrilled to talk about her personal life with Myles—even if it was a break away from the baby, the baby, the baby.

"But you're not so skinny anymore." His voice had dropped to a lower, more intimate timbre.

"You're voluptu—" He stopped, then added, "I never thought you were weird. Creative, yes. Head in the clouds sometimes, yes. Smart. Clever. Maybe even a little stubborn. But never weird." He glanced away, paused, as though considering his words.

"I have a confession to make," he said, and she was surprised to hear the thread of uncertainty in his voice. "Remember when I first met you at the plant? What is it now, nearly nine years ago? Before you grew up and I bit the bullet to branch off on my own."

She nodded, remembering all too well. The way her heart had tripped over itself to fall at his feet, the way she couldn't seem to make a coherent sentence around him when more than anything in the world she was dying to impress the dynamic, up-and-coming superdesigner of the hottest wheels on the road. She, along with every other female in the workplace.

"How could I forget?" she said. "My first job out of design school and I get assigned to your project. I was terrified of making a mistake."

"You only had to do rough drafts," he said with a chuckle. "Or they were supposed to be just that. Do you realize that you made quite an impression with those drawings of yours? I think the head of the art department was afraid of losing his job to a whiz kid."

"I didn't know that." Faith could feel a rosy glow spreading across her face. She'd felt so awkward then, so horribly unsure of her abilities. For so long she'd imagined Myles had only been kind, giving compliments to a green kid who looked up to him. "I wanted to prove myself, but I didn't think anyone really noticed."

"Oh, they did." His hand gravitated to her hair, and for a heart-stopping moment he touched it, then let go. "I noticed too. And not just the drawings."

Was she hallucinating? Hearing things? Did pregnancy affect a woman's brain so that she heard only what she wanted to hear and imagined something that had to be nonexistent?

"What?" She gulped, suddenly reduced to the twenty-one-year-old woman he'd first met, the one still trying to find out where she fit since she was a left foot and the world a right shoe. While he was older, worldly, established in his career and easy in his own skin, holding her enthralled and dazzled as if she'd stared too long at the sun. He was so far beyond her reach, she might as well have cried for the moon.

"I wanted to ask you out and I would have if there hadn't been a company policy against fraternizing. And, too, I thought maybe I was too old for you. You were just out of school and I was hitting thirty. I figured you'd think I was out of line, that I should act my age. Maybe even that wouldn't have made me back off if I hadn't met . . . your sister."

"Gloria," Faith whispered, remembering the shock of Gloria's news. That she'd met a man named Myles Wellington at the grocery store of all places, and once they'd started talking, one thing led to another and they went to a bistro for coffee. He even said that he knew Faith! And Faith, why hadn't she told anyone she knew such a marvelous man. He was witty, handsome, fascinating!

Never had she seen her sister so ecstatic. Gloria, the salt of the earth, as solid as a rock while she, Faith, tended to be as changeable as the sea. Gloria, the gentle nurturer who protected her little sister with a mother's vengeance whenever she jumped in with both feet without looking first. Gloria, who bit back unkind words when Faith was apt to heap on scalding epithets and shake her fist if a jerk cut her off on the exit ramp.

Gloria, the loving, demure preschool teacher with a porcelain-doll face who feared she would never meet the right man, get married, and have a dozen of her own. Faith, the outrageous dresser who wore her hair in the latest "do," danced until she dropped, and had to decide which date to keep since she'd already scheduled two . . . did something worthy of her sister.

She kept her mouth shut for once and committed the most unselfish act of her life.

"Anyway," he went on, "I started seeing Gloria. And then you quit your job. I never did understand that, Faith. Why you left, just like that, when you had a promising future where you were."

"I—I guess I didn't realize it was so promising at the time," she said faintly, still disbelieving the attraction had been mutual, even a little. "And Denver was a pretty place to live. It was a chance to start a life of my own. Away from family and school and . . . anyway I figured it was time for me to grow up and try to make my mark in the world." She shrugged. "Funny how you think you're all grown up and know it all. Then the more grown up you get, the more you realize how much you don't know."

"One of the great universal truths," Myles agreed with a shake of his head. "Imagine, Denver of all places, without a job and not knowing a soul. I wonder, would you do it all over again, knowing what you know now?"

Would she? As much as she'd loved her sister, would she give up another chance at the one man she'd never been able to forget, who set the standard so that every other man was doomed to fail?

"I didn't do so badly," she said, skirting her own unsettling questions. "My career means a lot to me." *Because it's really all I've had.*

"You've done well for yourself, which doesn't surprise me. But you were missed by a lot of your colleagues. And family."

And you, Myles? she ached to ask. *What about you? Did you ever miss me until you cried or dreamed of holding me in the night? Or did you ever have one failed relationship after another because you kept comparing them to the way someone else made you feel—a never-to-be lover who made you burn with no more than a casual brush of the hand, who made every other touch leave you cold and empty inside? Did you ever have to leave the room when we were together because it hurt too much to know it was never meant to be? Did you? Did you?*

"I missed everyone too," she said, while the memory of it all tightened her throat. "But it was the right decision to make. I think. A person can never be completely sure."

Myles sought her eyes, seeming to look for whatever it was she withheld deep in the reaches of her soul.

"Who was he?" he asked quietly. "The man in your sculpture?"

"It was a man," she confessed slowly. "A very special man."

"Was he the reason you left?"

"He had . . . more than a little to do with it."

"A lover, then?"

"No," she whispered. "I'm afraid he was married."

He hesitated, then drew her into his arms. Lightly. Companionably. But beneath the controlled exterior she sensed a tight leash on something building, something frightening because it was so powerful, so hungry; and because she was afraid she was imagining it.

"His loss," Myles murmured, and his voice took on that caressing timbre again.

"No." She gathered her courage and laid her palm over his cheek. Warm. Rough. Masculine. Infinitely better than she'd imagined. "No, Myles," she said. "The loss was mine."

Something flickered behind his eyes, something far more personal than compassion. And then she felt him slip a finger beneath the collar of her blouse, against the bare skin of her neck. He slid it around and released the strands of hair caught there.

She shivered. He tensed.

"I didn't mean . . . it's just that your hair is so pretty. It reminds me of . . ."

Gloria's, she silently filled in when he paused. *Before she lost it.* The memory, as well as the knowledge that Gloria might always stand between them, hurt.

"It reminds me of wheat before the harvest. The way it's not quite dark but has a hint of gold . . . like the sun kissed it."

Thank God he was holding her, because otherwise she was sure she would have ended up in a puddle of ecstasy on the floor. She slumped slightly, and her breasts connected with his chest, the beat of his heart matching the steady throb of hers. Heat flared inside her and spread until she could feel an ache low and poignant, that only he could create and soothe.

He was pressed against her belly. He was aroused—blantantly so. She couldn't stop the soft gasp that broke from her lips. He was so hard she could actually feel him pulse through the layers of their clothing. Then he made a sound that was low and harsh and gutteral as his body strained against her with a single, urgent rub.

The whys and wherefores and hows didn't matter at that moment, because right then heaven seemed to be making up for lost time. She closed her eyes with a long, rolling sigh. Loathe for the contact to end, she could feel her body reaching, shifting upward to urge him on at the same time that she struggled with the impulse to whimper, to seek his mouth with hers and slide her hand between their bodies.

"Oh, God," he groaned. "Oh—"

He abruptly thrust himself away. And there they stood, flushed, both breathing too fast and hard. Or maybe they weren't breathing at all, as they stared at each other with confusion and agony. Neither broke the thick silence that fell between them.

The diminishing rays of the sun slitted downward, and as if in accusation, they sparked against the gold of Myles's wedding band.

Faith's gaze was transfixed. How could she have disregarded it? As long as he wore that ring, he belonged to her sister, and she had no right to feel the hungry longing that lapped at her now. That had held her captive since the moment they first met.

She wanted him more than ever, but in that instant she knew Myles would have to free himself before they could go any farther. She felt impotent, her thoughts muddied by her own unresolved questions of loyalty.

Had he read her thoughts? Or had he simply followed her gaze. He lifted his left hand and touched the band. Her breath caught when he twisted it around in a gentle, caressing gesture. He began to remove it, then stopped.

The conflicting emotions were too strong for him to hide, or perhaps he was making no effort to disguise them. But what she saw in his face was enough to make her forget her own distress and ache to soothe his away.

Myles dropped his hands to his sides and moved

to another box. When he spoke again, his voice was rough, strained.

"Any problem with me opening this?" he asked.

"No," she answered in a wisp of a voice. "Open away."

Her attention gravitated to the half-uncovered sculpture. She repacked it, still trying to sort out the twists and turns of their encounter when Myles turned and fixed her with an enigmatic gaze.

"I know you don't exhibit your pieces, Faith, but I've always been interested in them. Maybe you'll show me that sculpture. After we've spent more time together and you feel comfortable sharing something that's . . . personal."

"That's possible," she said. She smiled at him then, cherishing his interest, his tenderness. But she could never forget the ring. Still the memory of his arousal flashed in her mind. He wanted her. *Her!*

He unpacked a small stained-glass piece she'd earmarked for the nursery. A prism of colors danced above his head as he held it up to the light.

"In fact," she added as her eyes locked with his and she felt the tug of remembered passion. "I'd say your chances are actually very good."

Four

Faith tapped the receiver. She'd been in Detroit for five days and had yet to place a call to Martin. Why she didn't want to talk to him, she wasn't sure, except that they'd been in cahoots in the well-intentioned scheme that had gone awry. Or maybe it was because any conversation they had would inevitably lead to the woman they had both loved dearly and lost.

Since her weekend encounter with Myles, she'd been trying to reconcile her conflicting loyalties—loyalty to her sister's memory and loyalty to herself. She wanted to get on with her life.

In spite of all her mulling about, she was still torn. She carried an irrational load of guilt that she was trying to steal her sister's husband. On the other hand, she thought that unrequited love just plain sucked.

With renewed determination, she reached for the phone and dialed. The law firm's secretary answered, and after Faith identified herself, she was immediately patched through to her cousin.

"Faith!" Martin exclaimed. "How are you? No, don't tell me. Barefoot and pregnant, right?"

Faith glanced down at her bare feet and grimaced. "Did anyone ever tell you that you're a sexist pig, Martin?"

"Yes," he said with a chuckle. "And I believe you were the one who told me."

"Only for your own good and because you can be so damn pompous, when you're not being irresistible."

"And I only put up with your abuse because I love you." He was silent a moment; when he spoke again, all playfulness was gone. "How are you, Faith?"

"I'm doing fine . . . actually better than fine. I'm in Detroit."

"Detroit. Well, what d'ya know. About time you moved back."

Her brows knitted in confusion. Martin hadn't sounded surprised in the least. She'd imagined that he would jump out of his leather executive chair with an exclamation-point reaction.

"You sound almost as if you expected as much."

He hesitated, then said matter-of-factly, "You'd planned to move before Gloria died, and I thought you might go through with it. Besides, Myles is here. I take it he knows and you've worked out a solution. Or at least I hope so. None of us needs a legal mess."

"A solution of sorts," she said, disconcerted by the conclusions that he'd leapt to. "Martin, I didn't tell him. Myles found the adoption papers in Gloria's strongbox. I thought we agreed that you would keep those."

"I did. She must have gotten a copy from the secretary. Hang on a minute, Faith." She heard him shuffling papers in the background, followed by the gruff message that he'd be in the meeting shortly. When he came back on the line, he said, "Sorry, but I'm going to have to cut this short. Just tell me one thing. How are you and Myles doing? Are you . . . I don't know how to say this exactly, but, are you helping each other get through this?"

"We're . . . coming along."

"I'm glad to hear it. I'd hate to think of the two of you getting into a custody battle. I know that's not what Gloria had in mind."

"What Gloria had in mind? What do you mean by that?"

"Just that—" He coughed, then as though he were making a lawyer's closing statement, he smoothly added, "Only the obvious. She loved you both and would have hated to see anything bad become of something that was meant to bring happiness."

"Yes," she agreed. "Gloria always wanted the best for everyone. I miss her terribly."

"Don't we all." After a few seconds he tacked on, "Do me a favor? Let me know if anything, uh, personal develops."

Faith pulled away from the receiver and stared at it as though it were Martin's face and he had just revealed a ghastly family secret.

"Faith? Faith, are you still there?"

"I'm here," she answered, then added under her breath, "Kind of. I think."

"How is pregnancy agreeing with you? No complications?"

Only emotional ones, she thought. "When I'm not in tears or pigging out, I love it. It's . . . miraculous."

"You'd do it again, then?"

"I'd do it again . . . and maybe even again." She wriggled her toes into the plush rug beneath her feet, relishing the image of conceiving a baby with Myles in a moment of love and passion. "Actually, Martin," she added, "I have to confess, I never much liked wearing shoes."

She hung up with a smile, feeling better for having talked to Martin. Yet she had the intuitive feeling that he was hiding something, and that his meeting had come at a very convenient time in their conversation. What would Martin have to hide?

"No nausea this morning?" Myles inquired, inhaling the aroma of the fresh coffee she handed to him.

"So far, so good. But I'm not pushing my luck by joining you." She pulled her white bathrobe tighter around her, feeling self-conscious.

It was the first morning she'd ventured down without getting dressed first. But now she wished she'd spent more time on her hair and added a subtle dash of makeup. Myles hadn't touched her since that weekend, and the seven days that had passed seemed more like years. The way she probably looked this morning, he might never want to touch her again.

"I'm glad you're not drinking coffee. From everything I've read, caffeine's not too good for the baby."

"So, you've been reading up on the subject, have you?"

"Everything I can get my hands on."

The hands in question were large, strong, and well cared for, she thought, despite the stubborn bit of grease under his fingernails. He got it from tinkering with his "toy"—a one-of-a-kind automobile he nursed and cajoled and cursed in his backyard shop.

"I like your suit," she said, shifting her attention. "It's very . . . European."

"I call it my corporate straitjacket." He chuckled. "Damn monkey suit. Almost makes me wish I was back where I started—on the assembly line with Dad right out of high school. I always did like the nuts-and-bolts end of the business. Good thing, I guess. My ideas and designs wouldn't have gone too far if I didn't know how to make things stop and go."

"You were on the fast track before you were twenty," Faith said, feeling a familiar pride. He was a self-made man, and she had great respect for that. "The name Myles Wellington was legendary by the time I hopped on."

"I don't believe in resting on your laurels or believing your own press. It's too easy to become complacent that way. A person doesn't have that luxury, especially one with only a high school diploma to fall back on."

"That bothers you?" she asked, surprised.

"Sometimes," he admitted with a shrug.

"But how could that bother you, Myles? You've actually done the impossible—broken off and formed your own independent line."

"We're small," he reminded her. "Still in our infancy."

"True. But competitive."

"I could get buried." He laughed. "I'm not exactly giving the big guys a run for their money, Faith."

"Not yet. But you will," she insisted.

"I'm glad that you believe in me, but only time will tell. At least I've got my chance, thanks to enough backers who didn't laugh in my face and call me crazy behind my back. I heard it all so often, I started to half-believe it myself. Continuing on became as much a matter of pride as realizing the vision."

"You're not a quitter, Myles, and those investors apparently knew genius when they saw it—that, and a chance to get in on the bottom floor of a potential gold mine. I know it was a struggle, but look how far you've come. The last I heard you were getting more orders than you could fill, and they haven't even rolled off the assembly line." She looked at him anxiously. "Has that changed, Myles? Are you having problems with the EPA or the distributors or foul-ups with production or—"

"We've worked through most of that, and the loans are secured. But even at that, we've got our share of difficulties. That's life. The same way people never outgrow their roots or their need for acceptance, no matter who they are or what they become. That's life too."

"You mean your upbringing and never getting a college degree to hang on your office wall?"

"That's part of it. Sometimes I feel like an imposter running a big corporation. I'm no Lee Iacocca in the making, no Henry Ford incarnate. Deep down I'm just an ordinary grease monkey. Hell, I was taking old cars apart and putting them back together before I was ten. Practically everyone I knew depended on the factory to put food on the table. That's a far cry from most of the MBAs who work for me."

"I imagine most of the MBAs who work for you wouldn't mind being CEO for a day," she countered.

"Yeah? Well, that's the other misconception that bothers me. To use an old cliché, it can get pretty damn lonely at the top. If things go bad and I lose it all, I'm left with nothing but a mountain of debt and a ruined reputation."

"But it wouldn't be that way. If the impossible happened and you did go under, I'd still be there for you. You're not alone at all, Myles."

The words were out before she could stop them.

He went very still, his attention locked on her. At that moment she was incapable of moving or speaking or managing more than a shallow breath. He pinned her where she stood as he looked over the rim of his cup.

Her hand rested on the countertop; he covered it with his.

"No. I'm not alone anymore, thanks to you." His

gaze drifted to her belly, and a warm smile touched his lips. "Your support means a lot to me, Faith. I'm not usually one for spilling my guts, but it helped to get some of that out of my system. When you've had to be a rock for a long time with no one to support you, it's hard to admit even a little weakness. It gets to a point where constantly needing to prove you're invincible becomes a weakness in itself."

"You're anything but weak, Myles."

"You're right, I'm not a weak person. But it feels damn good to know a woman who's strong enough to make me feel it's safe to show a chink in my armor."

The warmest feeling bloomed from within and rose up to her cheeks. "I'll treasure that, Myles. It's the nicest thing a man's ever said to me."

"As much as I'd like to think that's true, I find it very hard to believe."

Faith could feel her heart lift, her delight heighten. The scent of soap and aftershave filled her senses. He had a small nick on his jaw from shaving, and she longed to kiss it, or to lay her palm on his cheek. His hair was still a little wet from his shower, the dampness beckoning her to tread her fingers through it and capture the last bit of moisture between her fingertips as she cradled his head and urged his lips to hers.

She longed to grab the wonder of what they'd shared not so long, yet forever, ago, to make this perfect moment even more perfect. The niggling concerns, the horrible possibility that his need wasn't really for her but for the baby he wanted or that she simply made up for his great loss—no, she wouldn't think of any of that. She would concentrate on remembering the pulse of his arousal, the hum of mutual desire . . . and not consider that it could have been no more than a normal male reaction to *any* female after what she suspected had been a long period of celibacy.

No, she wouldn't let those possibilities steal her joy. What she had now was so much more than she'd ever dreamed possible.

"You are calling an obstetrician today, aren't you?" His lingering glance at her belly made her think he wanted to touch it. "I'm getting worried since you haven't seen one in almost a month. Take much longer and *I'll* call," he warned.

"I've already made an appointment with Dr. Laurentz. I understand she's very good."

"How good is she? I want only the best for you and the baby."

"Good enough to deliver another Taylor into the world, and that's good enough for me."

At the mention of her last name, Myles's jaw tensed. "Faith, I . . . there's something I want to talk to you about."

"Anything, Myles. What is it?"

"I . . ." He plowed a hand through his hair, mussing it provocatively. "You don't mind if I come along when you go, do you?"

The warmest sensation filled her heart.

"Mind?" She felt as though sunshine spread up from her toes. "I wouldn't mind at all. In fact I'd like it very much."

"Then that's settled." Myles returned her smile

and he seemed hesitant to break the spell. Then he hooked a finger through his mug and took another swig of coffee. "Faith, there's something else we need to talk about."

"Yes, Myles?" she said, finding this domestic morning banter very appealing.

"It's just that . . . what else do you have planned today?"

"I have a few places for lease circled in the want ads. Since you said it might take a while to find a good house, I thought I should get right on it."

"I'd rather you let me go along."

"You would?" Could it be that he would miss her? She wasn't above fishing to find out. "You're not worried that I'll get lost, are you?"

"Of course not. You pretty much know what areas to avoid, since you grew up around here. It's just that I want to have a say about where the baby's going to live."

"Oh. Of course, the baby." *Not me.* She found herself fighting the ridiculous impulse to cry.

Myles reached for his briefcase. At the door he stopped.

"I don't want to be a bother or anything, but if you have the time, would you mind calling the dry cleaner's and asking them to pick up a few suits I left on my bed?"

A vision of Myles's bed—the bed he'd shared with her sister that was now big, empty, and somehow haunting—flashed through her mind.

Oh, to share a bed with Myles, how she wanted it. But not that bed. Never that bed.

"Sure," she said with feigned brightness. "I'd be

happy to. In fact I need to get out anyway for some supplies, so I'll just drop them off myself."

"Are you sure you should be driving?"

"Of course. I'm just a little over four months."

"Okay, but be extra careful. And don't work too hard."

"I know." She sighed, then forced a smile to disguise her disappointment. "You're worried about the baby."

"About you, too, Faith. And by the way, did I mention that you do a lot for that bathrobe?"

As he exited the room, Myles took in the pleased expression on her face and held on to it, knowing it would help him face another grueling day. That Faith believed in him and would be there no matter what bolstered his confidence. Success was damn hollow when it couldn't be shared, and knowing Faith cheered for him in the wings fueled his determination to be the best he could be.

His step was light for the first time in a long, long while, and as he reached his personally designed roadster—which wasn't nearly as appealing these days as a station wagon—he realized that he had been whistling.

He felt . . . liberated. New. Faith had an inner fire, something that the primal man inside him responded to. Whenever he looked at her, he was gripped with the need to protect. To provide. To *mate* . . .

He'd more or less gotten over the jolt of their encounter, shocked but immensely relieved that she hadn't recoiled from him, had unbelievably urged him on.

Since then an edge of tension had emerged between them, intensifying the fantasies he couldn't escape, even in sleep. Especially in sleep. Nights were hell. Waking up in a cold sweat was becoming the norm for him.

But if that was the price he had to pay for having Faith near him, so be it. He didn't want Faith to leave. When they looked at houses, he'd simply find something wrong with each one and say that it was unsuitable for his child. He'd neglect to mention his more personal reasons.

Reasons that continued to plague his conscience. They were like an octopus. He'd slip free of its grasp just long enough to inhale the sweetest air, air that made him feel drugged—yet acutely alive—with the headiest sensation he'd ever experienced. And then another tentacle of memory or guilt would grab him . . . until Faith made him laugh or touched him or he glimpsed the evidence of his baby, and again he would break free and gulp air with the desperation of a drowning man. Sweet, heavenly air he ached to draw from Faith's soft, moist lips.

How could he feel this way? Didn't Gloria deserve more faithfulness to her memory? He'd been a good husband, a faithful husband; he would have gladly died for her.

But he was alive. And every time he thought of Faith, he was reminded of that. His loss was a fact, but he had to survive. More than survive. Live.

The time had come to bury his grief. He and Faith were having a baby, and Lord, did he want that baby.

Almost as much as he wanted Faith.

As he glided his hand over the steering wheel, Myles felt the band of gold bite into his finger with a familiar pressure. He'd worn the ring since the day he'd taken his vows, the vows that he'd kept.

To love and to cherish. In sickness and in health . . .

Till death do us part.

He took a sharp turn to the right onto an exit ramp, then drove straight to the cemetery, which he hadn't visited since bringing Faith home.

He got out of the car and trudged up the icy hill. There was no one to see the tears in his eyes. Tears he didn't try to stop as he worked his ring against the calluses that time and labor had earned.

And no one but the silent residents heard the catch in his throat as he carried on his one-way conversation with a tombstone marking a grave, where the grass awaited spring to thicken and grow.

Five

As they waited for her turn to see the doctor, Faith let her glance slide once more to Myles's left hand. A pale line on his ring finger contrasted sharply with the darkness of his skin. Nearly a week had passed since she'd first noticed the ring's absence, but the sensation of amazement, of hope lingered. That, and a heart full of sympathy for whatever struggle he must have gone through to make the break.

She wished she could comfort him. He'd been unusually quiet, seeming to draw into himself, touching her rarely, carefully, and with a sensitivity that felt like a unspoken need for understanding. She might have played a role in his decision, but she knew he needed to heal in private.

Perhaps he was almost there, and she prayed it was so. Today he'd been different, more his old self, and unabashedly excited about their trip to the doctor. The way he touched her today was also different—frequently, with lingering touches that felt tender yet assertive. Just thinking about it made her shiver.

"Faith Taylor? You can come back now."

"Thanks, I'll be right there." She put down a magazine containing the latest childrearing advice. "Myles, I'll be back in—"

"I'm going with you, Faith." He stood before she could finish, and offered his hand to help her up. "I didn't take off this afternoon just to be relegated to the waiting room."

"But I thought . . . I assumed . . ."

"I assumed you understood. I want to be part of this pregnancy from here on." He flashed her a wicked grin that knocked her off balance. "Just because I wasn't around for the conception doesn't mean I have plans to forgo the delivery."

"Mrs. Taylor? Dr. Laurentz has a tight schedule today, and we do have a few things to do first."

Faith could feel the blood rise to her cheeks. She'd had several prenatal visits in Denver, and she knew exactly what those few things involved. Disappearing for a specimen and changing into an exam gown behind a curtain while Myles waited to see her belly get measured wasn't her idea of getting more intimate in their relationship.

"Myles, really—"

"Look, Faith. I understand that you want some privacy, but I refused to duck out every time you get an attack of modesty. Considering what having a baby entails, I'd be left out until the nurse held Junior up in the nursery window." He took her arm and firmly propelled her forward. "Now, come on, I promise not to peek while you're changing."

Caught between an impatient nurse flipping open a manila folder and the stubborn set of Myles's jaw, Faith allowed herself to be led toward the scales.

On the way the nurse introduced herself as Diane. "And you're Mr. Taylor, I assume?"

"No, I'm *not* Mr. Taylor. But I *am* the father."

"Thank you for getting me in so soon," Faith cut in quickly. "I know a week's notice isn't much time."

"Usually it's not, but as far along as you . . . How much did you say you normally weighed?"

Diane jiggled the iron weight another quarter pound.

"One hundred and fifteen. And I'm five-seven."

"Hmmm. You're up twelve and a quarter pounds."

"Twelve and a quarter pounds!" she blurted. "How could I gain twelve pounds already? Wait, it has to be the shoes. I've still got—"

"Halfway to go," Myles finished.

"I'll look like an elephant," she groaned, fighting those blasted tears again. Twelve pounds! How could Myles ever find her attractive or desirable? Just when she'd thought that his recent change in attitude was because he was drawn to her as a woman, she had to go turn into a big, fat blimp. "Face it. I'm getting fat."

"No, you're not. You're beautiful."

Faith's attention snapped from the metal scales and collided with Myles's inquiring gaze.

He was waiting for her reaction, she realized with more than a little surprise.

She opened her mouth, but no words came. She could only feel warmth, the utter delight that he found her beautiful. The scales were wrong. She hadn't gained twelve pounds. She was weightless, floating.

Until Diane led them down the corridor.

"Nervous?" Myles whispered next to Faith's ear.

"Am I that obvious?"

"To me you are. Every time you get nervous, you do this little thing with your bottom lip. Like this."

She looked up to see him draw his bottom lip slowly between his teeth. It seemed unpardonably seductive in the clinical surroundings.

"I do that?" Was she having another hot flash? The room was suddenly so warm. "How do you know?"

"I look at your bottom lip a lot."

"You . . ." She couldn't seem to quit looking at his mouth. "You . . . do?"

The mouth in question curled into a pleased smile.

"You just did it again. Does that mean it's me who's making you nervous and not the doctor?"

The examining room door yawned open, and Faith looked from Myles to the table covered by a sheet of white paper. A shapeless blue gown was draped over it. The nurse was busy dragging out a cup, a monitor, and a tape measure.

"Both," she said in a strangled voice. She turned to him then with a plea in her eyes. "Myles, please, I don't want—"

"Enough said. I'll wait out here until you're ready." He touched her cheek with his fingertips, then tucked a stray curl behind her ear. "I'd really like to hear what the doctor has to say, and ask a few questions. If she needs to do anything that's too personal, I'll leave the room. How's that?"

"That's . . . fair," she agreed.

Ten minutes later she decided it wasn't fair in the least when Myles entered the examining room with an expectant smile and covertly gave her a once-over. She felt at a distinct disadvantage sitting on the end of the examining table with the unflattering gown gracing her less-than-perfect body. Her legs dangled over the sides, and a quick glance assured her they were turning a mottled shade of blue. At least they were shaved, she thought miserably.

"You don't have to look so amused," she muttered. "How'd you like to trade places?"

"I think the doctor might have a problem with that." His sudden cough was very suspicious. "Diane said we had about a twenty-minute wait, by the way."

Great! Twenty minutes stranded here afraid to move because she could feel the paper sticking to her bare bottom and didn't want to rip it. This situation was definitely bad for her blood pressure. A bead of sweat trickled between her breasts. She hated this. She wanted Myles, who appeared to be strangling a laugh and was still dressed in his impeccable suit, to share in her growing discomfort.

"What's so funny anyway?" she demanded.

"I'm sorry, it's just that . . ." He shook his head, and his mirth dissipated. He leaned close and murmured confidentially, "Can you keep a secret?"

"What a question, for you of all people to ask," she observed, knowing he couldn't possibly guess he was the deepest secret of all.

"Touché." He let his gaze drift from her bottom lip to her breasts.

She felt a quickening there. Then lower . . . lower.

"My secret is that this afternoon I looked at nursing gowns. I thought most of them were plain, but compared to this thing they were pretty darn sexy."

"You went shopping? For nursing gowns? You're not serious."

"Never more so."

"But why?"

"You said you planned to nurse." His gaze lifted slowly from her breasts. His eyes, as dark and somber as a midnight sky, were more piercing than she could ever remember. The quickening intensified to a quiver.

"Since you said that," he murmured, "I keep imagining my baby suckling you." He touched his finger to her mouth. "I'm also envious as hell."

Her first instinct was to bite her bottom lip. His finger caught between her teeth.

"I was hoping you'd do that." There was a gritty edge to his voice that matched the narrowing of his eyes. "But, please, don't feel compelled to stop there."

Her tongue seemed to have a curious will of its

own, and her voice was reduced to a small whimper. She tasted a trace of soap, which mingled with the faint saltiness of skin.

She probed the contour and taste and texture of his fingertip. He made a noise deep in his throat that was between a groan and a growl.

Without thought she responded, closing her lips around his finger. She suckled his finger with the hunger of a babe at the breast, with the sensual eroticism of two lovers in the heat of passion. Then there was the feel of his other hand working through her hair and moving against her scalp.

"I think you'd better stop," he said in a low, rough voice. "Because as it is, I'm burning to find out if the other things you do with your mouth are half as good as what you're doing to me now."

With reluctance, with a thrill of sensual confidence she'd never experienced before, she complied.

"Just what is it that I'm doing to you, Myles?" Her voice wavered slightly, but it was throaty, deep, aroused.

"Too much and not enough. Making me want to live so that I can endure more of this torture. Making me feel until I ache." He tasted his finger where the moisture of her mouth lingered. "Making me want to forget about being polite and subtle and worried about how you'd react if I did what I've been dying to do to you."

"Why don't you do what it is you've been dying to do, and find out?"

Her heart was pounding so hard she wondered if

he could hear it. This wasn't the man who broke an embrace when his body called to hers or who solicitously inquired how she'd slept and insisted she eat the meal he'd prepared; and she wasn't the woman who yearned in silence and doubted her ability to make him long too.

"It might start with a kiss, Faith, but believe me, it won't end there."

He pinned her with a gaze that reflected the starkness of his need.

She felt as though she were seeing him for the first time. She clung to his desire, exulted in it. She couldn't let it go, not after waiting year after barren year.

"Where would it end, Myles?"

"Don't you know? Here." He placed her hand over his heart. It beat heavy and quick. He slid her palm down the crisp white shirt covering his hard, broad chest, then over his belt of thin leather and the smooth, chilled texture of the buckle, and then lower . . . lower still . . .

"And here."

She uttered a short, muffled cry. The shock, the thrill, the utter disbelief of where he had led her to touch him were almost enough to make her beg him to take her right there.

She knew they had somehow cut through the insurmountable obstacles of who they were and what had brought them there and were now confronting the bare truth of what they could be.

He pressed her hand over the straining thickness hidden within his tailored dark trousers, then curled her fingers into his groin. His breath left him in a low, gutteral moan, and then quickly he pried her hand away.

"And here, Faith," he whispered, this time touching her. His voice rough with emotion, he laid his hand over her belly, and she could feel him shake. "Here."

"Myles." She laid her hand over his and made no effort to restrain the tears. Where he touched her she felt a fluttering.

His face was transformed with shades of desire, and the torment of unsatisfied need. His eyes met hers in wonder, and a slow smile spread in understanding.

"Did you feel that?" he asked. The fluttering sensation again. "Faith—"

"The baby," she breathed, feeling it move within her for the first time. She'd always known it was there, but the movement, telling her it was truly alive and that it was growing inside, left her in awe and strangely humbled. "My baby," she said, feeling laughter and tears mingle in her throat.

"No, Faith," Myles said, beaming. "*Our* baby."

Moments later the doctor knocked on the door and found them in a joyful embrace, both of them laughing, with tears rolling freely down Faith's cheeks and Myles's hand resting protectively, possessively over the blue gown covering her belly.

"That's what I love about my job," Dr. Laurentz said after explanations were made. "There's nothing more wonderful than the birth of a baby. It makes up for the down sides of my profession."

Faith and Myles exchanged a look that said they knew firsthand of those down sides, but even the memory of tragedy and loss couldn't dim the rapture of what they'd shared.

The doctor went over Faith's file and asked a few routine questions, then picked up the monitor. She instructed Faith to lie down. Myles quickly moved to her side, helping her to lean back.

A sudden, irrational fear gripped her. What if something was wrong? What if the doctor couldn't get the heartbeat?

Myles took her hand and squeezed it. "It's okay. Remember, we felt the baby move." His eyes shone with lingering delight and a silent understanding.

"How did you know what I was thinking?"

"Because you went straight for the bottom lip, sweetheart."

Sweetheart! The endearment sang through her veins, making her forget her discomfort and the self-consciousness she had expected to feel with him standing there as the nurse pushed the gown up to her waist and tucked the sheet around her hips.

As the doctor applied the cold gel to Faith's exposed abdomen, Myles held her hand tight, and she could feel the encouragement and support he willed to her.

"Can I look?" he asked, and because he had cared enough to ask first, she found that she didn't mind.

"Only if you don't laugh." She caught her breath when the monitor made contact with the gel and began to glide over her stomach. "My tummy's not what it used to be."

"Unfortunately I wouldn't know any different,"

Myles whispered next to her ear before he shifted his attention to her slightly rounded middle.

She watched anxiously for any sign that he found her unappealing to look at and breathed a sigh of relief when he smiled warmly before sending her a glance that shone with paternal pride. He focused on the monitor as the doctor rolled it first this way, then that, but leaned down long enough to murmur, "I don't know how you were shaped before, but I can't imagine a prettier sight than this."

She was still glowing when Dr. Laurentz suddenly said, "I've got it!" and turned up the sound until a swishing noise filled the room. Underlying that was a quick, hollow beat.

"Hear that? It's your baby. And he's got a strong, steady heartbeat."

Faith clutched Myles's hand tight and a sense of such joy, of reaching beyond herself and touching heaven, caused a sob to catch in her throat. She didn't care if she cried, it was so wonderful, so perfect, she didn't care if the whole world saw.

Myles returned the pressure of her grip, then lifted her hand to his mouth. He pressed a soft kiss on it before impulsively brushing his lips over hers.

"Thank you," he whispered, his own eyes brimming with unspoken emotion.

Before long, Dr. Laurentz was putting away the monitor while Diane efficiently wiped off the slippery gel before Myles gently lifted her up.

"Now, let's see, you plan to breast-feed, right?" Dr. Laurentz asked.

"Yes," Myles and Faith answered in unison. They looked at each other, and a sensual spark arced between them.

"You need to toughen your nipples of course," stated Dr. Laurentz, matter-of-factly. "I imagine they're fairly sensitive."

"Um . . . yes, they are."

Myles quirked a brow; his smile broadened. "What do you suggest for that, Dr. Laurentz? Is there anything we can do to . . . work on getting them ready?"

"Oh, sure. She can go braless and let the material brush against her for a few minutes each day or use a rough towel and rub them until they're not so sensitive. Be sure to keep them conditioned. Lanolin is good for that. Of course you've got a while yet, Faith, so if you want to wait, you can."

Myles bit his tongue to keep from commenting. Faith's cheeks were a very attractive shade of pink and getting pinker by the minute.

"But I do want you to keep up a routine of regular exercise," she added. "Nothing too strenuous, but walking, even swimming is good. And of course, you need to watch your diet. Twelve pounds isn't too bad considering you were a little underweight to begin with, but you've got a long way to go, and in those last few months the pounds can add up."

"Don't worry, Dr. Laurentz," Myles assured her. "I'm watching Faith's diet. We'll be sure she eats properly."

"Good. Now, have you discussed delivery? You

can change your minds along the way, but I always recommend Lamaze classes in the last trimester. If you're interested, I have all the pertinent information." She nodded to Myles. "A lot of husbands coach their wives."

"But he's not—"

"I've already got my stopwatch," Myles cut in. He narrowed his eyes on Faith, silently daring her to say more. She didn't know it yet, but he was going to be her husband before their baby was born. It was a deeply personal cause, to ensure his child was legitimate.

But his personal cause had taken unexpected turns. How could he convince Faith and himself they could be married in name only if he kept having this gut-wrenching, heart-pounding reaction to her? He couldn't. Whatever rational ideas he'd come up with in Denver had bit the dust once Faith was in his blood.

"Now," Dr. Laurentz said, "any concerns or questions about sex?"

"Yes," Myles said as he looked straight at Faith, who fidgeted nervously on the table. "Sex is definitely a concern."

"Faith's in excellent health and shows no signs of risk. Medically I see no reason to curb a healthy sexual relationship. Be as intimate as you want, as frequently as you like, until the last few weeks or so—just as long as no complications arise. Only, once the baby begins to grow . . . well, most couples manage to work around that."

"Considering what we've been working around, I don't think that'll seem like much of a problem."

Myles chuckled while Faith made a strangled noise and gripped the sheet at her hips. The doctor looked from one to the other, then gave a small shrug.

"I'm here if you need me. Call if you have any abdominal cramping or vaginal bleeding. Otherwise I'll see you in a month."

"We'll be here," Myles assured her. Alone again, he braced both hands on either side of Faith's hips. "So, how did I do?"

"You did fine," she retorted. "Better than fine, *coach*. Even after I told her about . . . about the IUI, you led her to believe . . . to believe—"

"That we're, umm, intimate?"

"Yes! And not only that, you didn't let me get a word in edgewise. I just kept sitting here while the two of you discussed me like I didn't have a tongue to speak for myself."

"But, Faith, you and I both know you do indeed have a tongue." He reached around and untied the top ribbon of the gown. "A very talented tongue, I might add. Though even an expert like yourself can always use some extra practice."

"Myles!" she gasped, capturing his hand when he began to undo the second tie.

"And I think you should know that I can be a real taskmaster. As your coach I'll expect you to limit your practice to me. Especially since—"

"Myles, what are you doing? For heaven's sake . . . Myles! Stop that! That's the last—"

"Especially since I consider it my solemn duty to help you work on things such as breast-feeding." He pulled her gown slightly away from her neck.

Just far enough to press a kiss to her throat and feel the giveaway leap of her pulse.

"I, for one, think we should give that top priority," he murmured seductively. "Rubbing and massaging your . . . sensitive areas sounds like very serious business to me. Certainly not to be neglected."

"Myles." Her neck arched back, giving him access.

"And as for your diet . . ."

She moaned as he tongued the warm hollow of her throat. The eyes that met his were glazed, aroused.

"My diet?" she said in a distant voice.

"Mmm, yes. I definitely plan to monitor your diet. The main course today is a triple hot fudge sundae. A scoop for you and baby and me."

"And . . . dessert?"

He trailed his fingers up her bare back, then speared them through her hair. He fixed her with a purposeful stare.

"For dessert, my dear, you get me and only me."

Six

"White," she insisted. "I have my heart set on all white."

"Pastels," he countered. "Or maybe something like that cute little thing we saw in the store with red and blue teddy bears dangling around it."

"That was a mobile, Myles." She smiled at the musical nursery lamp he'd allowed her to carry up to her bedroom. He was busy situating a huge stuffed giraffe and fussing with the layette they had selected together after feasting on the hot fudge sundae he'd promised.

"At least we agreed on the baby bed."

Bed. Her gaze automatically turned to the big four-poster in the middle of the room and she tried hard not to think about what might or might not happen now that the evening was drawing to an end. Her stomach twisted tight with nerves, and her gaze skittered away.

"I think the baby should feel like royalty with a

brass bed and a canopy," she added, while her anxiety climbed a notch.

"The baby *is* royalty." His brow furrowed. "You're sure he won't bang his head on that thing?"

"Not with bumpers. *White* bumpers."

"I can see you're going to be stubborn about this." He took the lamp and hooked it up beside the bed. "Turn off the lights and we'll make sure it works. By the way, I like those pastel bulbs you found." He switched on the lamp and sent her a simmering look that didn't coincide with the tinkling lullaby. "They're very soft. Romantic."

She watched Myles sit on the edge of the bed. He held his hand out to her. She took it.

"Stand there," he said, urging her between his parted thighs, then whispered something against her stomach. She could feel his breath through her clothes. She swallowed hard and exhaled on a shallow gasp.

"What are you doing?"

"Talking to the baby," he said, then placed a soft kiss where he'd whispered. "Why are you shaking, Faith?"

"I—I don't know. I think I'm scared."

"Of me?"

"Of . . . us." She let him pull her onto his lap; she could feel the tautness of his muscles beneath. Was he shaking too? Was that what she felt as he urged her arms around his neck? "I'm afraid of what's happening here."

"And what's happening? Say it, Faith. Let's get this out in the open where it belongs. Starting with how it feels when I do this." He threaded his fingers through her hair and exposed her neck. His lips were soft, moist. She felt the flick of his tongue against the erratic pulse of her throat. "Does it feel good?"

"Good," she breathed. "So . . . good."

"Then why are you pulling away?"

"Because . . . because . . . Myles, I don't know." The last word caught on a sob. What was wrong with her? She'd waited for this forever, and now that it was happening she was a total mess. What if it didn't work out? What if she did something wrong? What if . . . what if after it was over, Myles realized it was only the heat of the moment and he was sorry for or felt guilty about what they'd done. What if . . . ?

"Is it Gloria?" he whispered into her hair.

"I feel . . . it's crazy, but I'm afraid I'm cheating on her." She made the confession even while her muscles clenched and she moved closer to the heat of his body and tentatively stroked the corded strength of his neck. "Maybe most of all, I'm afraid you'll decide that this was a mistake and then it'll become awkward with us. I couldn't bear that, Myles."

"The only mistake I could make with you is pretending what's happening between us isn't really happening. No one can absolve us of what we're feeling but ourselves, and the only way we can do that is to accept that we're the only ones who can be cheated. Gloria's gone. It's time we both said good-bye."

He lifted his ringless hand to the light. "I've been saying it for the past week. You have to do the same or we're not going to be able to deal with our relationship."

"And what is our relationship, Myles?"

"That's what I'm asking you. What your doubts are . . . and your fears."

"I do have fears," she admitted. "I fear that I'm convenient and you're lonely."

"And male?" He stroked her leg with his fingertips, then massaged her inner thigh. "I've had seven women offer themselves to help 'ease my loneliness,' in the past month. I wasn't even tempted. I didn't want them."

"But you want me?"

"I think that's apparent. Just as I think we both know this is inevitable." His hand moved to the buttons of her blouse, then hesitated. "But I have to tell you, it's been a long time since I was single. I'm not sure if I'm going about this the right way. I feel like an awkward kid who's afraid of making a fool of himself by making the wrong move and offending the woman he's about to go out of his mind to touch."

"I'm not offended," she murmured, melting inside with the honesty of his confession, with the miracle of his wanting. Taking the leap, knowing this was the only way they could possibly break free of the past and embrace the future, she leaned forward until his hands were pressed against her chest. "I want you to touch me."

His breath left him in a ragged sigh. "I'd love to see your breasts."

In answer she reached for the first button, but

her hands were damp and trembling so hard, she couldn't slip it free.

"It's reassuring to know I'm not the only one with a case of the shakes," he said with a low, seductive chuckle. He brushed her hands aside and began to work the buttons with a slow sureness that made his claim of awkwardness seem without merit.

One. Two. Three. And then there were none. He parted her blouse and she watched amazed as he closed his eyes with an expression of ecstasy and nuzzled her cleavage while he unlatched the front clasp of her bra.

She could feel the warm dampness of his breath, the cool wisp of air against her skin as he peeled off her bra and dropped it to the floor. He pulled away and their gazes locked with charged passion straining at the leash. And then slowly, deliberately his gaze moved downward.

He made a sound of delight, of hunger. "Oh, Lord," he whispered, "you're too beautiful. Too beautiful to look at and not taste."

His mouth skimmed over her flushed breasts, which felt fuller, more sensitive and aching than she could bear. Still she endured. She endured the sweetest agony she'd ever dreamed possible when his tongue glided over her, then swirled and probed the buds that were distended and feverish.

"Ahh," she cried softly as he closed his lips around her.

"Do you know how you taste?" He nipped her gently before lightly grazing each nipple with a day's growth of beard. "Like a forbidden fruit in a garden that just had the gates thrown open. I've been looking and wanting, and now that I've got you, I can't get enough." He lifted his head, and she saw the deepness, the openness of his greed.

"Then take more," she whispered. "More . . ." She clutched blindly, gathering his hair into her fist. There was a small hesitation before his lips brushed over hers, and their open mouths met.

She could hear their labored breathing, could smell the scents of their bodies mingling with heady desire. Urgently she slid her hands between them and tried to strip him of the shirt that robbed them of the feel of flesh against flesh.

Without breaking the kiss he jerked his shirt off. The buttons scattered over the bed and onto the floor, but she was only vaguely aware of the popping sounds, the whisper of a garment falling next to hers. He brushed his chest against her, and she reveled in the roughness of his hair.

He shifted until she lay on the mattress and he was beside her. Tasting faintly of the Scotch he'd had earlier, his mouth continued to work against her own in a voracious taking and giving.

How long they mated with tongues and tiny bites of slick, hard teeth, she had no way of knowing.

With a final plundering of each other's mouths, he broke the kiss. She was afraid to open her eyes, afraid to let a measure of reality spoil the dream. But then he kissed each eyelid, and said, "Open your eyes. Look at me. There's something I need to see."

She couldn't deny him that, she couldn't deny him anything, so she did look at him. What she saw was almost staggering and all but singed her with its heated intensity.

"What do you see, Myles?"

"Something better than a fantasy. A woman who wants me as much as I want her." He wedged his hand between her knees. "A woman who needs to be touched as much as I need to touch her."

He moved his hand slowly upward and she could feel herself giving way to the insistent pressure of his palm. Close to the juncture that was crying for him, he stopped and kneaded her inner thigh.

"Do you want me to touch you?"

She nodded her head in a short, jerky affirmation.

"Then say, 'Touch me, Myles. Touch me there.' Let me hear your voice so that I know I'm not dreaming."

"Touch me . . . there. Please, touch me everywhere."

She was surprised she could speak through the pounding in her ears, in her heart. Inside her . . .

"Oh, oh . . ." Who was saying the single word over and over? Was it her, or was it him, or were they both uttering the moan of ecstasy?

"I feel you," he said in a low, rough voice. "Even through your panties I can feel you. You're moving against me. Do you ache, Faith? Am I making you ache?"

"Yes," she sobbed quietly. She could feel her hips lifting, her legs parting, seeking release while praying this spiraling peak would go on forever.

"I can't bear to see you hurting," he murmured next to her ear before tracing the shell with his tongue, then suckling her lobe. He nursed it even as he worked her hose and panties downward. She felt the shift of the bed as he kicked them aside. Then his fingers found her as his mouth took hers. Tremors. Her body sighing, weeping for more.

"Tell me how to make the hurt go away," he commanded gently at the same time that he stroked his fingertips over and around her, playing her body with a merciless accuracy. He stopped at the threshold and pressed without breaching. She arched up in silent entreaty, but still he withheld filling the emptiness.

"Please, Myles. Don't . . . don't make me beg."

"I want you to beg. I want you so far gone you're begging me not to stop. Not now, not ever." He pressed himself against her, moving in a rhythm that matched the sleek entry of his fingers.

She jerked upward, welcoming the unfamiliar sensation that plunged her deeper and farther into a world of intimate knowledge that was theirs and theirs alone.

"What are you doing to me?" she suddenly cried as he pushed deeper with a tempo that was slow and then furious. "What are you . . . I can't take much more of this. Please, Myles. Please—"

"I'm hurting too." He quickly led her hand to his groin. "Feel me hurt too."

She did feel him. And she also felt the hurt of their bodies, the agony of their souls. They were healing together, fusing their strength and mending themselves with this terrible passion that was tearing them to pieces, then putting them back together as no longer two, but one.

Through the cloth of his pants she could feel him pulsing and straining against her. She fumbled with his zipper, and with an impatient growl he opened it for her.

She was unprepared for what greeted her, for the hungry urgency of his immediate, rapid thrust. Her fingers wrapped tightly around him, and she cherished his flesh, the incredible warmth of his skin.

"Make love to me," she moaned. "Make love to me now."

"No," he groaned against the tangle of her hair. "Not yet. Not until . . . let it go, Faith. Let me feel you melt in my hand."

She had no answer as his fingers pushed inside her, driving her on and on until she was plunged into utter darkness.

"Myles," she cried frantically, blindly searching for his mouth, clutching him to her while she pleaded for him to take her now.

She opened her eyes and met his, slitted with a wild, dark fury. He was suddenly on top of her, his arousal sliding sweetly over her folds.

His fingers laced with hers, and he held her arms spread in helpless surrender on the bed.

"Why?" she whispered.

He brought her hand to his mouth and tenderly kissed each finger, closing his eyes as he struggled with his own unsatisfied yearning.

"It's too soon for us, Faith." He skimmed his lips over hers, then lapped at her tears. "I had to . . . to have you, at least this much. We took our first step. But we need more time before we run."

"It wasn't enough, Myles. I only took."

"You took what I wanted you to have. And I'll take the rest. When we're both ready."

"When we're ready?" she repeated, uncomprehending. She was struggling with the confusing mix of ecstasy and distress. Surely he hadn't guessed . . . but he'd touched her there. Could he have somehow realized—no. It had to be something else.

"I don't understand, Myles."

"Don't you? The urge is so strong, it makes me want to forget to be gentle, to forget your body's not just yours anymore."

"You're afraid of hurting the baby?" She'd forgotten, and as if she needed a reminder, she felt a slight fluttering inside. The baby bound them, yet kept them apart.

"A little. But that's not all. It's so intense with us, Faith . . . like nothing I've ever experienced before. I know once we finish what we've started, I won't be able to sleep without you, and I for one will want a lot more than what you might be prepared to give."

"And what is that, Myles? Whatever you want, it's yours for the taking."

He studied her closely, then shook his head. "Not yet. I'm not one for asking until I'm certain I'll get what I ask."

Before she could pursue whatever it was he held back, he stroked her once more and winced. "Promise you'll still respect me in the morning?"

"I've always respected you, Myles. Always—"

She stopped. His brows drew together and he repeated, "Always . . . what?"

She swallowed hard. "Always cared for you."

"I want you to do more than care." He rolled off her and stood beside the bed. The evidence of his unsated desire gleamed with a sheen of moisture as he struggled with his pants.

His immodesty was a little shocking, and she found herself wanting to study at close range what she'd only felt, though not closely enough.

"Don't look away," he said. "I want you to see me. To see what you do to me."

He stopped until her gaze was fixed where they both wanted it.

"Tell me, Faith, do you like what you see?"

"I—" She gulped in the air that suddenly seemed in short supply. "Yes, I like looking at you." Her lips felt suddenly dry; she wet them with the tip of her tongue. Then she did what she wanted more than anything in the world to do and leaned forward to press her lips to him. She was rewarded with a hoarse, masculine growl.

"Only in my fantasies," he groaned. Myles took a sudden, short step back and zipped his pants. She felt a terrible sense of loss. "You're killing me, Faith. With any luck I'll dream about that kiss and maybe wake up feeling better than I do at the moment. Though, chances are, I'll only feel worse and question my sanity for leaving it at this."

He stared downward, and Faith followed his gaze. Her skirt was hiked up to her hips and her breasts pouted. Her skin was still bathed in a rosy glow of passion and tinted with the peach glow of the nursery lamp.

She reached for the coverlet at the end of the bed, but Myles took it from her and shook it out. He tucked it beneath her breasts before parting with a lingering caress to each one, then a slow, deep kiss.

At the door, with rent shirt thrown over his shoulder, he turned. "That man, Faith, the one you sculpted but didn't want me to see?"

"Yes?" she said anxiously. "What about him?"

"I hate him. I keep wishing I could find that bastard and treat him to a knuckle sandwich for hurting you. Not only that, but for taking a piece of your heart."

For a long time she stared incredulously at the door. Myles was gone, but she held fast to his expression as he'd said those words—one revealing jealousy and fierce possessiveness.

Shaking herself out of a state of stunned jubilation, she reached for a pillow and buried her face in it.

She inhaled his scent and pressed her mouth against the feathered down to muffle her whoop of joy.

She was leaning against the counter making the morning coffee when he entered the kitchen on bare feet. Bracing a hand on either side of her, Myles leaned into the small of her back and nuzzled the hair against her neck.

"Mmm, smells good."

She went still, one hand on the faucet and the other gripping the stainless steel pot.

Her laugh was a little nervous. "The coffee does smell good," she agreed.

"Who's talking about the coffee?" he murmured next to her ear before biting it playfully. He was pleased that she shivered in spite of the heavy terrycloth robe.

"Umm . . . did you sleep well?" she asked.

"No. Lousy is more like it. What about you?"

"Not too good either."

"I'm glad. As they say, misery likes company."

He felt her throaty chuckle against his lips, a chuckle that echoed suspiciously of relief.

"No regrets?" he asked, just to be sure.

"No. What about you?"

He reached past her and cupped warm water into his palm as his other hand loosened her robe.

She gasped as the water trickled a criss-cross path over a single ivory breast.

"Put the pot down and turn around." When she didn't immediately comply, he extricated the handle from her grip and pivoted her with a firm grasp of the waist. His hands fit neatly into the curves that had expanded but were still shapely enough to test his limited control.

When she faced him, her eyes were wide and more than a little hazy.

"The only regret I have is waking up alone and wishing I could see you naked in the full light of day." He bent his head and lapped the water. A single bead trembled at the bud of her nipple; he sipped it, and when she sighed and wrapped her hands around his head to pull him closer, he tugged the robe loose.

He let his gaze rove hungrily over the full length of her body. She flushed an alluring shade of pink.

"You're not disappointed?" she asked with an anxiousness she couldn't hide. "I'm getting plump."

"Disappointed?" he repeated in disbelief, then laughed, amazed she could still be self-conscious about her changing body, especially after the intimacy they'd shared. "If I were any more disappointed, I'd short-circuit a fuse. In fact I'm tempting fate as it is." He drew her robe closed. His hands tensed at the lapels, and he pulled her up to him with a sudden, urgent demand.

Their lips were eager. Any lingering questions or stray doubts either one of them might have had were burned away by the searing fire of a single, scorching kiss.

"Now, tell me," he demanded, "do you need any more convincing of just how disappointed I am? Careful how you answer, Faith, because I'm dangerously close to laying you on this countertop and taking what I didn't take last night."

"No, you convinced me," she answered shakily even as she moved against him.

Careful, he warned himself, desperately clutching at the frayed edges of his rational mind. *Be very careful here. You've got too much at stake to risk taking too much too soon. Just because she wants to sleep with you doesn't mean she'll marry you too.*

Myles summoned his last ounce of control and

moved away, not trusting himself to be within an arm's distance of her.

"Where do we go from here, Faith?"

Her eyes came wide open and she stared at him in confusion.

"Where? I'm not sure, Myles. I don't know exactly where this leaves us."

He couldn't look at her and not rush back to finish what he'd deliberately started. His gaze wandered around the room, then zeroed in on an open newspaper on the table. He went to it, to see if his disturbing suspicions were true.

"Damn," he muttered under his breath. More houses? Even after last night? He stifled a curse. He'd run out of legitimate complaints five houses before. "What in heaven's name is this, Faith?" he demanded, tapping the classified ad circled in red.

"It's a house for lease," she said evenly, turning to pick up where she'd left off with the coffee. "I found several possibilities," she added. "Maybe you'd like to look them over with me after work today."

"The hell I will," he growled before he could consider the wisdom of his response.

"I beg your pardon?"

"I said, 'The . . . hell . . . I . . . will,'" he enunciated.

"But I thought you said you wanted to go with me."

"That was then. This is now."

"Have you got a problem, Myles?" she asked uncertainly, moving toward him with an empty cup.

"Yes, I do have a problem." He took the cup and set it in the middle of the paper with a *thunk*. Her stunned expression was enough to make him sufficiently recover himself and come up with an excuse for his outburst. "What I mean is, we already have other plans."

"We do?"

Glancing at the red ink, he hardened his resolve to see his plan through and pulled her firmly, insistently into his embrace. He threaded his fingers through her hair.

"Didn't I tell you? We have a dinner engagement with one of my biggest backers." Time was running out faster than he'd expected. He needed to set the mood and he needed to do it quick. "But after that I know where there's a band that plays only slow dances." He could feel her relax, lean into him until he groaned with the effort of restraint.

"And after that . . . ?"

"After that," he said through taut lips, "we talk about why we're not looking at houses."

Faith burrowed her face into the warmth of his chest, hiding the pleased smile curving her lips.

Seven

Faith sucked in her gut. The full-length mirror was unforgivably honest in its assessment. The short gold-lamé dress showcased her legs to their full advantage, but it hugged her middle, though once it had shimmered and freely swayed.

"I love you, baby, but you're not doing much for my ego," she muttered with an affectionate pat to her rounded tummy.

Slipping into a matching pair of heels that were snugger than she remembered, she paused when she heard Myles on the other side of the wall shutting a drawer. She wished she could watch as he went through his dressing ritual.

Did he put on his shirt before his pants, or his tie before his shoes? A thrill rushed through her as she thought of undressing him in reverse. The prospect was becoming more real with each day they lived together.

Smiling, Faith applied a sinfully-rich ruby shade

of lipstick. He didn't want her to move into a house of her own. If she could only be sure his motives had nothing to do with the baby. She hated the niggling doubts of uncertainty, her own insecurities, which persisted despite the intimate turn of their relationship.

Where did his feelings for her begin and those for the baby end? If she wasn't carrying his child, would he want her as much, or care so deeply, or come close to a hissy fit because she kept looking for another place to live?

"Oh, stop it, would you?" she grumbled. "Quit acting like a woman who's jealous of her own child and so unsure of herself, she doesn't want to share."

After all, she'd been sharing him for so long, she should be used to it by now, shouldn't she? No, dammit. She needed him to want her for herself alone and for no other reason. Was that so much to ask?

A tap at the door caused her palms to sweat. Stealing a last glimpse at the mirror, Faith had to admit she did have a certain appeal, despite motherhood's generosity.

She grabbed her matching sequined bag and opened the door.

Myles stood with his elbow braced against the frame. His gaze traced downward from the seductive pile of her upswept hair to the flushed expectation of her glowing face and the sensual shimmer of the sexy dress that looked better on her now than when he'd seen it two Christmases before.

He whistled, his anxiety over how he was going to propose before the night was over, momentarily forgotten. "Lady," he growled, "you are a knockout. I'm starting to wonder if it's your personal mission in life to push me over the edge."

"Like it?" She turned a full circle.

He caught her by the waist and pulled her against him. The lamé at her bosom connected against the starched front of his tuxedo shirt. His hand slid up her back and toyed with a coy curl brushing her nape.

"I love it," he murmured. "Just like I love—"

You. The word lodged in his throat with a jolt. For a moment he was too stunned to fill in the gap. He'd almost said he loved her. *Was* he in love with Faith? Was that what all these new emotions and possessive instincts were about?

As she continued to stare at him wide-eyed, her lips parting as her breath caught with a soft, inviting gasp, he grappled with the possibility. His gaze settled on her lips, lips he wanted to nibble and devour until her lipstick was smeared and he licked the remains from her mouth.

"Your hair," he said roughly while he flirted with a pin holding it up. "I love your hair. But I'd love to take it down even better."

What did he see before she quickly covered her reaction with a teasing smile? Disappointment? Had she wanted more? Or had he simply wanted her to want more and imagined the softly sighed "Oh."

"I could wear it down, if you want."

"Leave it up. I can spend the night thinking about taking it down later."

"You make 'later' sound like a promise." She brushed her lips over his. "Or maybe a threat. You said we had to talk tonight."

"We'll talk, all right. But I'm learning you're better persuaded with the kind of language that doesn't require an abundance of words." His hands lowered to fan over her buttocks, and he pulled her to him.

She rubbed against him with a feline grace and he heard her purr of desire as he fit his tongue into the warm hollow in her throat.

"Lord, woman. I'd be jealous of all the men in the restaurant if I didn't know you were carrying my baby."

Her motions stilled and he looked at her quizzically. "Did I say something wrong?"

"No," she said faintly. "I . . . I just realized if we don't leave soon, we'll keep your people waiting. Let me grab my coat and we'll go."

Myles stared after her, uncertain what had turned the heated tide. He wasn't any closer to an answer as he took her purple coat and drew it around her with a kiss, which she didn't return with ample fervor.

Once in the roadster, he glanced over at Faith, who stared out the window with only an occasional half-smile in his direction.

"You're quiet."

"Just thinking about my work," she said evasively.

"I know your work's important, but my concern is that it doesn't interfere with your health."

"My health's fine," she retorted. "Quit fussing over me like a mother hen, okay?"

She studied the passing buildings with undue interest, avoiding his startled expression.

"Tight fit in this car," he said, hoping to ease the slight tension. "Once the baby's here, I think we'll need a bigger one."

"I have my sedan. It has plenty of room for me and a car seat."

Me and a car seat? So much for his power of persuasion. His grip tightened on the leather-bound steering wheel.

"Don't I rate a space?" he asked with an edge of frustration.

"That depends," she said a bit shortly herself. "I usually drive my own car, and I'm sure the baby's things will take a lot of room."

"What the hell is that supposed to mean?"

"It means we both know this baby comes first, and you can park your buns in the trunk if you want to join us."

"I don't like the sound of that." He flipped off the CD player and in the sudden charged silence looked away from the road long enough to shoot her a glare. "You make it sound like the baby's all yours and I can tag along for the ride."

"Aren't you?" she said peevishly, returning his glare.

"For crying out loud, Faith, you're talking non-sense. We agreed this was *our* child. Not to mention what's happening between us."

"Us?" she sniffed.

"Yes, *us*. What do you think last night was about?" He stopped the roadster short of the restaurant entrance where the valet stood waiting. "I've got the hots for the mother of my child. If that's a crime, I'm guilty. But you share the blame—strutting around in that bathrobe that's straining at the bust, wearing that dress that's going to have every man ogling you tonight so that I won't be able to keep my mind on business."

"I think you're giving me too much credit." Her lips tilted slightly upward, and he fought the urge to kiss them shut. Then she added hesitantly, "I doubt every man has a yen for pregnant women."

"This one does." He discerned the fading of her tentative smile. What was with her? Pregnant women! Who could figure them? Was she still feeling self-conscious about her figure? The heck if he knew, but it seemed as good a reason as anything for her mood swing.

"I like you pregnant," he added, hoping to put things right. "What's more, I'm thrilled as all get out that it's *my* baby. I can't wait to show you off to Larry and Carol."

Larry and Carol, I'd like you to meet my . . . my . . . sister-in-law? The woman who's carrying my baby? No, wait a minute . . . . This is Faith. You'll notice she's expecting, and I'm proud to say it's mine, but please disregard the fact we're not even engaged. And I'm sure good manners will dictate you won't mention how shocked you are since my loss is still recent.

Good manners, bull, Myles thought. They'd be curious, if not inquisitively rude.

"Myles?" Faith said when he continued to stare grimly at the entrance. "What's wrong?"

"Just getting a grip."

A sleek limo passed them with a short honk. The valet opened the door, and a silver-haired woman draped in mink and diamonds accepted his hand. A balding gentleman in a dinner jacket with a cigar between his teeth emerged on her heels.

"Larry and Carol," Myles muttered. "Why couldn't they be late as usual?"

"You don't sound too happy they're here. Are you worried about something?"

No, Faith. Nothing like that. I'm just trying to come to terms with how the devil we're going to handle this whole situation tonight. I've been so wrapped up with how I'm going to ask you to marry me, I didn't think ahead. Not to mention that my plans are getting more botched by the minute, and there's next to no time to salvage this crazy mess I don't understand any more than I understand when I started falling in love with you.

"Look," he said, sighing, while the other couple signaled in their direction. "I don't know what I said or did or how we ended up getting into an argument. Whatever it was, I'm sorry. I'll try to make it up to you, but you're going to have to level with me. It takes two to make things work and figure out what went wrong. Whether what we've got is only for a night"—he took a deep breath—"or a lifetime, I don't want to waste it with petty misunderstandings."

Their gazes locked. When she laid her hand over his, he hoped it was a sign of encouragement. Anything to ease his apprehension so that he could focus on getting through what was bound to be one helluva strained dinner.

"I'm sorry, too, Myles," she said. "I don't know what gets into me lately. I'm so manic, I'm driving myself crazy. I didn't mean to take my . . . my nervousness out on you. Especially tonight. I told you I would always be there for you, only so far I'm not doing a very good job."

"Wrong. You're the brightest spot in my life— you, and Junior." Ignoring his backer, who was about twenty feet away but was scrutinizing them with increasing interest, Myles brought her hand to his lips and pressed a lingering kiss there. "Think we could call it a truce and start the night from scratch?"

"Why don't we just edit out the ride and keep the rest?"

"Sounds like a winner to me. But just one question before we tackle dinner with these two. You're sure it's just nerves or hormones? You're not upset with me about something else?"

"I'm sure. It's not your fault that I want—" She glanced down at her stomach and stopped short.

"Not my fault that you want what? Spit it out, Faith. I'm not moving the car until the air is cleared."

"Nothing, Myles. Let's pull up. They're coming this way."

"Tough." He had to get to the bottom of this before things could unravel even more. "They can bang on the windows for all I care, but we're not budging until this is settled. Business can wait. Anything that's affecting us personally can't."

Faith jerked her attention to the oncoming couple and rushed on. "All I meant was, it's not your fault I want to impress them. I'm afraid the dinner will be awkward."

Myles grimaced. "Awkward? I think that's a fair assumption. But we'll get through it—together. And as far as impressing anyone goes, you're worried about nothing. *I'm* impressed, and that's all that counts."

He stamped his assertion with a firm kiss on her mouth, then drove the roadster forward. He waved at Larry, who had visibly clamped down hard on his stubby cigar while Carol nearly slumped out of her mink with an expression of incredulity.

They'd seen the kiss and were obviously shocked. Too bad, Myles decided. He wasn't going to act as though Faith was less to him than she was. Even if the other couple had adored Gloria. Lord only knew what they were thinking. Once they got a gander at Faith's stomach, questions were going to be blunt. The whole surrogate fiasco was none of their concern, but he'd be damned before he'd pretend the baby wasn't his. He was as proud as punch and didn't give a tinker's damn what anyone else thought.

Except for the issue of legitimacy. It raised the hackles on his neck just thinking about his child being considered a bastard.

"Are they nice?" Faith asked anxiously as the valet sprang forward and opened her low-slung door.

"Nice. Conservative. And rich enough to be outspoken without worrying too much about stepping on someone else's toes." His gaze lowered to her belly as she stepped out. "They're also very family oriented. Ask about their grandkids, and the conversation won't run dry."

"But what if they ask about—" She gestured to her midsection. "What will I say?"

"Leave it to me, sweetheart. I'll handle them. Just relax and let me take care of any explanations."

He opened his door, but before his feet could touch ground, Carol and Larry had reached her.

"And you are?" they were saying while neither seemed capable of looking beyond Faith's stomach. Myles quickly hurried around to drape a reassuring arm around her shoulder.

"I'm—" She bit her bottom lip. "I'm Faith. Faith Taylor. You must be Carol and Larry."

"Not Gloria's sister?" they said in incredulous unison.

"Larry and Carol," Myles said, "this is someone you've heard a lot about. Please say hello to—"

"Your sister-in-law," Carol supplied as she continued to shake her head. "Though what I saw a minute ago couldn't pass for casual, and really, Myles, how could you . . . with Gloria barely—"

"How are your grandchildren?" Faith interjected frantically. "I'd like to hear all about them."

Everyone went silent. Larry chewed his cigar

and studied her with undisguised curiosity. Faith instinctively hugged her middle. Carol opened her mouth, then shut it. A muscle tensed in Myles's jaw while he gritted his teeth.

"Save your judgments for someone else," he said with quiet control. "We've had a lot happen to us that doesn't bear sharing with other people. But you can rest assured that despite appearances, Gloria was never cheated." Myles pulled Faith close to his side while he fixed the couple with a warning stare. "That said, I'd like you to meet Faith. Not only is she having our child"—he took a deep, steadying breath—"she's going to be my wife."

Eight

Three pairs of eyes locked on Myles. He desperately wanted to see Faith's reaction, but at the same time he was afraid to look.

She tensed beside him and gasped aloud.

Larry saved Myles the trouble of digging himself in any deeper by extending his hand and grasping Myles's in a firm, gentleman's grip.

"Congratulations," Larry said. He nudged his wife and said, "Carol, don't you have something to say?"

"Yes, of course," she said distantly, seeming to be in shock. "Congratulations. We hope you'll be very happy. And . . . um, I suppose congratulations are in order on your apparent . . . uh, great expectations. Assuming I heard right. You did say it's yours, Myles?"

"Carol," her husband said in a warning tone.

"Definitely mine," Myles asserted before venturing a glance at Faith. "And so is Faith. Aren't you, dear?"

She was staring at him in disbelief. His eyes begged her not to dispute him.

"Yes," she murmured faintly. He tightened his hold as she swayed slightly and nearly lost her balance. Her teeth began to chatter. "Could we go inside? I'm feeling a bit chilled."

Myles solicitously patted her hand, which did indeed feel icy, and led everyone inside the restaurant.

Myles was quick to help her off with her wrap. Seizing the moment for a private word, he whispered, "Please, just go along with it. Ad-lib when you have to, don't let her get you alone in the ladies' room, and nudge me under the table if you're in a jam. Please, Faith. Do this for me. I have my reasons."

"Whatever they are, they'd better be pretty damned good. How *could* you, Myles," she whispered sharply. "You could have at least given me notice you were going to pull such a ridiculous stunt."

"Sorry. I didn't know it myself until you were out of the car and about to get pummeled by Carol's nosy questions. You have to admit I didn't get us in such dire straights all by my lonesome. I'm just doing my best to clean up the mess."

"Well, you certainly could have fooled me. Your great idea to clean up the mess just thickened the gravy. I'd like to strangle you for putting me in this kind of a spot."

"But you'll back me up?"

She hesitated, and his hands tensed at her shoulders.

"I'll back you up. But you'd better watch it under the table because any nudge you get from me is going to be a kick in the shin."

He smiled politely, realizing they were being watched, and kissed her sweetly upon the cheek.

"Just try to remember we're a happy couple."

"Right. Madly in love."

The sarcastic quip was a brutal strike to his own newly realized emotions. He tried to harden himself against it, but failed miserably.

"Speak for yourself," he said in defense.

"If you'd just give me a chance for once, I would."

Her whispered retort was sharp, but he thought he discerned hurt in the depths of her stormy eyes. The hurt wasn't hers alone. Her outrage was justified, but dammit, did she have to act as though the idea of marriage to him was so distasteful? She'd just have to develop a taste for it, by God, because marriage was what he wanted and marriage was what he would get.

When the maître d' sat them, Myles made it a point to situate himself next to Faith, with the other couple across the elegantly set table.

Myles reached beneath it to squeeze Faith's hand in reassurance, but Faith avoided him, folding her tapered fingers together, her long, ruby-tinted nails contrasting vividly against the linen white.

They were saved the necessity for small talk by being handed menus.

"Would you like me to order for you, Faith?" Myles inquired.

"No thank you," she said too politely. "I'll order

for myself this time." She proceeded to study the menu with concentrated interest.

"Wine or before-dinner drinks, sir?" the maître d' asked.

"I'd like a Manhattan," Larry said. "My wife would like wine. Chardonnay."

"Thank you, dear," Carol said.

"Scotch for me, please," Myles said. "Sparkling water for—"

"I'll have half a glass of wine," Faith cut in. "I'd like the Chardonnay as well." As the waiter left, she leaned forward and sent Carol a pleasant smile. "It's my favorite too."

"Excellent choice," she agreed.

"Faith," Myles said in a low voice, "you know you shouldn't be drinking since you're—"

"But Myles," she protested with a gracious wave of her hand, "the doctor said an occasional small glass wouldn't hurt. And besides"—she nodded to the other couple, who were watching them with great interest—"I'd like to toast to our . . . engagement. Especially since we have the pleasure of sharing the evening and our very recent news with Larry and Carol."

"Recent?" Carol repeated. "So I take it you haven't been planning this long?"

"Oh, no," Faith answered. "We were engaged very recently. You didn't possibly think that we would, well, under the circumstances you surely realize I'm not nearly as far along as I appear. I'm showing very early, is all. What Myles said is true. Neither of us would have done something immoral and hurt a person we both loved very much. Fate simply intervened at a very crucial time."

Myles breathed a silent prayer of thanks. In spite of her anger, she was helping them maintain their moral dignity.

"I'm glad to hear that," Carol said, apparently satisfied with the explanation. "We thought the world of your sister. She's missed by many. Please accept my belated condolences."

"Thank you, Carol. Time helps."

Carol nodded her head in approval. "So does having something as joyful as a wedding and a baby to look forward to. I love babies more than anything."

"Then you'll have to come hold ours once it's here. Won't she, Myles?"

She was setting him up! Faith was trying to make him squirm since she apparently thought his trumped-up marriage plans weren't going to come to pass. She expected Carol to see their child but still no wedding ring and, my oh my, wouldn't he have some explaining to do then.

When he didn't immediately reply, Faith made good on her promise and stepped on his foot.

"Of course," he agreed smoothly, managing not to grimace when she increased the pressure. "We'd love for you to pay us a visit." He smiled conspiratorialy at his partner, who removed her heel and was suddenly busy trying as discreetly as possible to remove the hand sliding intimately up her thigh. "You'd like the nursery. We're doing it all in white. Except for a teddy-bear mobile I set my heart on."

Faith turned to him, pleasant surprise and physical distress heightening the color of her cheeks. Point for the home team, he thought victoriously, and gave her a wink.

"How delightful. I can't wait." Carol accepted her glass, which was delivered promptly. "Really, Myles, you shouldn't make such a fuss over Faith wanting to join us for one drink."

Faith patted his hand. "That's okay, he's just being protective. Myles is very doting when it comes to my health. Most women should be so lucky." Faith accepted her wine and nodded in the other couple's direction. "By the way, our engagement is so recent, I can hardly believe it myself. Except for me, you're the first to know about our wedding plans."

Carol clapped her hands together and exclaimed, "What a nice thought!"

"I see you found a charming young woman, Myles. You're a fortunate man to strike gold not once but twice." Larry lifted his glass. "It must run in the family."

"I'll drink to that," Myles said, fighting the urge to down his glass in a single gulp. He squeezed Faith's thigh beneath the table one last time and whispered, "Though at the moment it feels more like acid than gold."

Faith's response was a defiant tilt of her chin and a triumphant spark igniting her eyes.

"A toast," Larry announced. "May your joys be many and your sorrows few."

Their glasses clinked.

"I'm ready for some joy," Myles said candidly. "I

think we've both had enough sorrow to last a lifetime."

Carol hesitated. "I . . . I apologize if I was, shall we say, insensitive earlier. Whatever happened along the way, I know you grieved over your loss."

"I appreciate you giving me credit for that." Myles took a long swig off his Scotch. "But thanks to Faith, I'm getting past that. The future's not dreary anymore, but something to look forward to."

He decided the liquor must have gone to his head, because he was leaving himself wide open for Faith to scrape another piece out of his heart.

She remained quiet, however, as she took a small sip of her wine.

Myles clamped down the impulse to take the glass away. Faith glanced at him and murmured, "Don't worry. I made my point. I don't even want to drink it now."

A round of appetizers arrived, and the shift of attention on the other side of the table gave him the chance to whisper, "Still mad at me?"

"You bet I am," she whispered back. "But you can relax. I promise to be good until we leave."

"You are good. A spitfire I don't know how to handle yet, but good in more ways than one."

"We'll see how good you think I am once we're alone. This spitfire's liable to torch you, so you'd better handle with care."

The challenging set of her mouth set off fireworks that sparked from his head down to his legs. He wanted to kiss her crazy until she quit fighting him and cried for mercy.

If he didn't cry for it first.

"By God, Faith, I think I've met my match."

"Flint and steel?" Her expression softened in direct contrast to her whispered words.

"More like friction and combustion." He sensed a little easing of her resentment when she smiled in spite of herself. "A lot like last night," he murmured seductively. "I keep remembering the way you cried out my name and whimpered for more."

Faith's cheeks turned scarlet, and he had the satisfaction of hearing the sharp intake of her breath.

"When is the wedding?" Carol suddenly asked.

"We haven't set a date yet—"

"Next month—"

They answered at the same time.

"Which is it?" Larry speared a shrimp into his cocktail sauce.

"Both," Myles answered, shooting a beseeching glance at Faith.

"Umm, right. Next month, but we don't know which day."

"By all means let us know when you do," Carol said. "I love weddings almost as much as babies."

"But you can't," Faith hastily interjected. "I mean . . . well—"

"It's going to be small," Myles supplied.

"Yes, small. Just the immediate family."

"Oh." Carol sighed. "Well, perhaps we can see the pictures."

While the appetizers were cleared away and the entrées served, Myles muttered, "Thanks, Faith."

"You owe me, buster. And I can't wait to see the

pictures either. Maybe you can just cut and paste and switch faces in your old album."

She reached for her wineglass and took a drink without looking at him.

He was stunned. Not just by the insensitive remark but by the underlying anger that seemed to go deeper than the awkward situation he'd gotten them into.

Dinner progressed with dinner talk, business talk, and more questions about the wedding. Faith was charming, an entertaining conversationalist, and resourceful in fending personal questions, though she spoke to him directly as little as possible. He felt a distinct coldness in the way she shifted away from him as far as her chair allowed.

Larry and Carol were obviously impressed. Faith managed to make up for his lack of participation, his own answers reduced to monosyllables while his mind remained stuck on Faith's bitterness.

Her unspoken hostility became more untenable with each passing minute. When he'd had all he could take, he interrupted the conversation.

"I hate to be a killjoy, but I think it's time for us to call it a night."

"Why, Myles? I'd like to hear more about Carol's grandchildren."

"Because," he said in a tight voice, "you need your rest." He got up and pulled her chair back, firmly grasping her elbow until she followed suit. "Say good night, Faith."

Her back stiffened, and he knew she was madder than a hornet.

"Yes, Myles, I do believe you're right. I am feeling tired all of a sudden." She kept her tone polite, and he had to admire her poise. "Thank you for a lovely evening, Larry and Carol. I'll look forward to more dinners like this."

The sarcastic remark went unnoticed by the older couple, who quickly returned the seemingly gracious comment. Myles smoldered.

"I'll take care of the bill on our way out," he insisted, ready to run Faith out of there at a fast trot.

"I wouldn't hear of it." Larry stood and shook Myles's hand in parting. "Just consider it an early wedding present."

"Thanks," Myles said with as much politeness as he could muster. "We'll do that. But next time's on us."

"Let's make it soon," Carol told him. "I want to hear more about Faith's artwork. It's so nice to have someone to talk to while you men talk cars and money into the ground. And again, congratulations. I know you'll be very happy."

"Ecstatic," Myles gritted out.

"What's your problem?" Faith demanded as he marched her out the door.

"You," he said curtly, signaling for their car.

"But why, Myles? I kept my end of the bargain. I thought you'd want to thank me for being the perfect future Mrs. Wellington."

"I'll thank you to keep your mouth shut until we get home. You've got some explaining to do."

"If anyone's got explaining to do, it's you," she retorted, dropping her icy politeness.

The roadster stopped in front of them, and Myles tipped the valet.

"Great wheels," the young man said enthusiastically.

"Yeah, great," Myles said, for once unable to care less about promoting his line. Nudging Faith, he muttered, "Get in."

She stiffly obeyed, sweeping past him with haughty grace before he slammed the door shut. While Myles was on the way to his side, a Mercedes pulled up behind them, and Martin got out, dinner partner in tow.

Before Myles could pretend not to notice them, Martin called out.

"Myles," he said, introducing his date as he pumped Myles's hand. "How are you? I was going to call, but you saved me the dime. Just wanted to let you know I'm headed for Europe."

"Vacation?" Myles asked, pretending interest. The only thing he was interested in was getting Faith alone and having it out. "Take lots of pictures," he added shortly, remembering Faith's earlier retort, which was as confusing as it was maddening.

"Not that kind of trip," Martin said, oblivious to the tenseness around him. "Big opportunity with a big firm we're joining forces with on a limited scale. We're branching out internationally, and . . . hey, you're not interested in all that stuff. But I'll be gone for a few months as a liaison."

"Be sure to call when you get back." Myles curtailed his desire to be rude and cut him off.

"Hey, is that Faith in there?" Martin leaned past

Myles and waved. "Wow, do you look sensational. How's the little mother-to-be?"

"Terrific, Martin. Simply . . . terrific. Get Myles to tell you about our big plans."

Martin looked from Faith to Myles as they glared at each other. Martin backed up, apparently coming to the realization all was not terrific.

"Big plans, huh? What's up, Myles?" he added, beginning to look uncomfortable.

"It's a surprise. When you get back from Europe, we'll let you in on it."

Faith audibly snorted with disgust.

Martin cleared his throat. "I'll look forward to it. I think. But at least I'm leaving on a happy note," he added, vainly trying to improve the mood. "The little one should be here by the time I get back. Got a name picked out yet?"

Myles dropped his facade. His face went stony.

"Good-bye, Martin," he said shortly. "Enjoy Europe."

"Thanks, I—"

The door banged shut with a resounding thud, and the roadster leaped forward over the asphalt.

Faith turned around to see a disconcerted Martin staring after them.

"You didn't have to be so rude," she charged. "You embarrassed him in front of his date."

Myles stared straight ahead at the road, his hand clenching and unclenching over the mahogany knob of the stick shift.

Silence was the only answer she got, and it thickened with each passing mile. The tension between them was stretched so taut, she felt as though fingers wrapped around her throat. She was chilled to the bone with an ominous foreboding of what was to come.

Risking a glance at Myles, she saw the profile of the man who had battered her emotions, had shredded her pride, had thrust a horrible farce upon her, a farce that had mocked her heart's deepest and longest held dreams.

Nine

"Get in the house," he ordered, flinging the front door open.

Faith kept her back rigid as she brushed past him. She was so angry. And hurt down to her soul.

"I don't think we should talk tonight," she said as evenly as possible, trying with all her might not to let her jumbled emotions and heightening anxiety show.

"Yes, tonight. *Now.*" Myles booted the front door shut, and it closed with a harsh, resounding finality.

"I don't think so, Myles," she said quietly. "We're both too distressed after a strained evening. Let's just say good night as civilly as possible and talk with clearer heads tomorrow."

"I have no intentions of being civil. And I don't care to let all hell break loose as it's about to, where we are. Head to my study while I make a drink, and get ready to take me on."

"You just proved my point. Good night. I'm going to bed."

Faith turned for the stairs, but before she could take a single step, she felt his fingers clamp tightly around her arm, then snap her around to face him.

"You asked for this, so don't try running away. Go to the study, or else . . ."

"Or else, what?" she challenged, refusing to let him intimidate her.

"Or else I'll simply follow you to your bedroom." His gaze lowered to her bosom and his eyes narrowed. "And I really don't think you want that, Faith."

"Are you threatening me? You wouldn't dare—"

"I dare a lot. And frankly, I'd love to hear you beg after having your nails sunk in my back half the night."

"Don't give yourself that much credit, Myles."

He pulled her against him and thrust a hand into her hair, loosening it from its pins, while his head lowered to hers.

She tried twisting away, knowing just how vulnerable she was to him. A primitive passion made her body respond immediately to his hardness pressing between her thighs.

"Stop it," she said urgently, trying to push him away at the same time her body rebelled and greeted his upward thrust with an answering movement. "I don't want you."

"I think you do. So let's find out."

Myles locked her against him. He insinuated his hand beneath her dress and found her heat. His fingers slid easily against her. She tried not to cry out, but she did, her legs buckling.

"That's what I thought," he said, pressing deeply inside her. "I'd never resort to force with you, Faith, but then again we both know I'd never have to."

"Please," she whimpered. "Please . . ."

"Please, what? Take you on the floor, against the wall? Or up to the bedroom you were so eager to escape to? We can do all of that, but not before questions are answered." He slowly withdrew his hand.

She wanted to cry—in frustration that he'd left her aching with the need for release, with hurt pride that he'd made her succumb so easily. She was angry with herself for letting him win. Keeping that anger in mind, she was able to gain a semblance of outward control, even though her breathing was still close to a shallow pant.

Not trusting herself to speak, she strode toward the study. Once inside, Faith prowled it restlessly, trying to think, trying not to give him an edge by getting more unnerved than she already was, and avoiding a portrait of her sister on a carved oak credenza.

Myles entered the room, his coat off, black tie dangling, tuxedo shirt a quarter unbuttoned and revealing a portion of the chest hair that had caressed her breasts the night before. The drink in his hand was generous. She declined the sparkling water he offered with a quick shake of the head, her unbound hair brushing her shoulders to remind her with a sensual pang of the way he'd loosened it.

By silent, mutual agreement they kept a physical distance between each other. Myles took a gener- ous swig of his drink while he wandered over to the credenza and opened a drawer. Casually he took out a photo album, flipped it open, and held it out for her examination.

Faith's heart seemed to skid to a halt as her gaze locked on the picture of a wedding party: Gloria in her white gown, beaming and radiant, Myles look- ing pleased and much younger, a dashing, hand- some groom. He was smiling and looking at . . . *her.* Faith. Her smile looked strained, her complex- ion pallid. And her eyes were focused on Myles, revealing sadness. Longing.

How could he look at this and *not* know?

"We'll start with this. If you want to make good on your earlier suggestion, I've got scissors and glue in my desk drawer."

Her stomach bottomed out as if she'd just been dealt a bodily blow. Her words, born of anger and agony, came back with clarity. She felt as if she'd spit on something holy.

She couldn't look at the photo and dropped her gaze. Only once had she seen the pictures, when good manners dictated she subject herself to look at the proofs the happy couple had selected. Next to the wedding it remained one of the worst mo- ments of her life.

"Don't you have something to say?" he de- manded. "Or maybe some artistic guidance on how we should go about doing this."

He quickly moved around to his desk, taking another gulp of the Scotch before setting the glass on the wood with such force the liquid sloshed over the rim. He opened a drawer and rummaged around before finding the necessary tools. Holding up the scissors, he offered them to her.

"Come on, Faith. Let's get started. You cut. I'll paste."

"Stop it, Myles!" she cried miserably.

"Just a little snip here, a little snip there and we'll patch this baby together."

"I can't—oh, God, please. Enough!"

He threw the scissors down.

"What's wrong, Faith? Artistic prerogative? You want to do it by yourself? Okay. I'll just sit and watch."

Her legs were shaking. Forcing herself not to drop her face into her hands and weep, she commanded her unsteady feet to take one step at a time until she stood in front of the credenza. Her hands were trembling as she closed the gaping album.

"I'm sorry," she whispered, unable to bring herself to look at him, feeling the biting glare of his eyes fixed on her bent head.

"Are you? Are you really?"

"Yes!" she said. "Of course I am. It was a horrible thing for me to say."

"It was, Faith. And totally unworthy of you."

"All right, Myles. I'm ashamed I let my temper get the better of me."

"Is that all it was? Temper?"

She made herself look at him levelly. With des-

peration she sought to protect her emotional na-
kedness, her dark need for secrecy.

"What else could it have been? I was angry. I
lashed out. I'm sorry if I hurt you."

"You did. You hurt me deeply."

She looked away, cringing inside, hurting for
them both. But mostly for Myles, for inflicting a
wound on the man she loved more than life itself.

"It wasn't . . . intentional." Unable to stand the
censuring silence, she asked, "Why didn't you just
tell them the truth, Myles?"

"What, that you were a surrogate for Gloria, and
leave it at that? Or maybe just pretend you weren't
pregnant at all while Carol shot questions like
hoops?"

"You could have let them think what they wanted."

"Oh, just act like it wasn't mine, then. What kind
of man do you take me for, Faith? I could shout to
the world you're having my baby while you're
trying to hide it like an out-of-wedlock minor."

"That's ridiculous." She raised her chin up and
glared at him, all of her horrible suspicions boiling
to the surface. She couldn't ignore them anymore.
She *had* to know.

"Do you know what I think, Myles? You want a
baby maker, not a woman. You want me because
I'm carrying your baby, not just for myself. Go
ahead, admit it."

"That's not true. I *do* care about you. Both of
you."

"You couldn't prove it by me. It's always the baby
this, the baby that. Never just about us."

"Maybe if I could quit worrying about my child

being born illegitimate, I'd have a lot more room in my brain to think about just us."

"That's it, isn't it?" She smacked her forehead as though a light had just come on. "How stupid of me not to guess. You want the baby to have your last name, don't you? Don't you?" she accused.

"Of course I want my baby to have my last name. Joint custody and written permission to use it on the birth certificate don't cut it either. I provide for my own. As far as I'm concerned, a man who doesn't own up to his responsibilities—especially a wife and child—isn't fit to breathe. I couldn't hold my head up if I let that happen. It turns my stomach to think about my child being born a bastard."

"The only bastard around here is you, Myles Wellington. You made me think you wanted me, when it was nothing but an act to get me to sign on the dotted line."

His eyes glittered with fury. "I haven't lied to you about my feelings to get my way."

"Does that mean when you came to Denver, you didn't have plans to do just that?"

Her breath caught, waiting . . . waiting . . .

"Yes," he said, flustered now. "No. I mean at first maybe, when I thought we could keep it platonic, I was going to get you to agree to a short marriage—in name only. But that changed. I didn't just want the baby to have my name. I'd hoped you might want it too. Only you just keep throwing it back in my face."

"And only because you didn't offer it to me first."

"Not offer it to you first?" he repeated. "Do you

care to clarify that statement?" His eyes narrowed to a slit.

"No! I—" How could she have said such a stupid thing? Faith blanched, then said in a strained voice, "You make me feel . . . incidental. Icing on the cake in a nice, tidy two-for-one package. Face it, if it weren't for the baby, you wouldn't have come for me. And for that, I almost wish it was any man's baby but yours."

"How can you say such a thing?" he said sharply. "After we nearly drowned in disease and death, we're given this incredible miracle like it was a kind of light leading us to the end of a black tunnel, helping us to find each other and make it through."

His eyes sought hers, piercing and full of troubled emotion. "Together, Faith. Not you and the baby. Or me and the baby. The three of us surviving. Committing. Being a family." He shut his eyes, sighing tiredly. "No wonder you never got married, woman. You make it so damned hard for a man to propose."

The ground seemed to open up and swallow her whole. She was suddenly dizzy, trying to keep her balance, hanging tenuously to the edge of the world by the strength of her nails.

"You . . ." she whispered. "You mean . . ."

"What do you think I've been trying to get to all night?" He looked down at her. His eyes were guarded as though he were waiting for a rejection. "I want you to marry me. For the baby, yes. But in this case, Faith, it's the baby that's . . . incidental."

She was shaking. She could feel tears streaming from her eyes and running down her face. His fingertips traced them as his expression turned tender, expectant.

"You . . . you want to marry . . . *me*?"

"You. Sleep, fight, love, grow old with me."

"I—" her voice caught on a sob. "I don't know what to say."

"Say yes, Faith. A simple yes will do."

She threw her arms around his neck and buried her face against his chest, rubbing her tears into the warmth of his skin, the crispness of his hair.

"Yes," she said, the word muffled. She raised her head, her face beaming with joy, and cried ecstatically, "Yes!"

A slow smile spread from his lips and ended in a laugh.

"I could strangle you for making this so difficult. I feel like I've just trekked down a hot path through hell. The scenery's lousy, and the sound effects are even worse."

"You want to marry me," she said again, not caring if she was babbling. "When? When do you want to marry me?"

Myles tilted his head, considering. "What say . . . next month."

"Only we don't have a date picked out yet." She chuckled.

"We could . . ." He paused and grew serious. "We could send Carol pictures."

Her mouth trembled. "I'm so sorry for what I said. Forgive me, Myles."

"Not only forgiven. Forgotten." He nodded toward the album. "I took that a little too far. If it bothers you, I'll pack it away."

"No." She looked from the album to Gloria's portrait, feeling for the first time unthreatened, able to accept. "She's part of your life. And part of mine. I think it would be very wrong of us to pretend she never existed."

"We exist." His hand lowered to stroke over her stomach. On cue, the fluttering came. Myles cupped her face and whispered, "We do exist, we three."

Their mouths met, hungry and gentle, injured and mended, seeking assurance and receiving it. Their kiss was fire and pure spring water. *Life.*

"Dance with me," he murmured.

"I'd rather make love."

"Who said we couldn't do both?" He threaded his fingers through her hair and moved sinuously against her. "The dance I have in mind starts with music and you in my arms, but it ends between the sheets."

Ten

He picked her up effortlessly and moved down the hall to the stairs. Her arms were looped around his neck, her fingers stroking the corded muscles. When he stopped at the open door of his room, she tensed.

"Is something wrong?"

Faith looked from his heavy-lidded gaze to the massive bed. She shook her head in apology. "Not . . . not here, Myles. It's—"

"I should have realized. Not very perceptive on my part, I'm afraid."

She touched her fingers to his lips, soothing him. "I understand. Don't feel bad."

"I'll move it to the guest room." He caught her lips in a sweetly fierce kiss. "How would you like to pick out a new one tomorrow? Our first piece of furniture—it'll be like starting new."

"A wedding present? From you to me?"

"From us to us." He turned and carried her to

the next room, relieved that the strained moment hadn't cast a shadow on their joy. He was absolutely drained, and he knew Faith had to be too. They needed sustenance, not old reminders.

He moved through the darkness of her room until he reached the side table with the nursery lamp.

"Do you mind?"

She reached down and fumbled for the switch. They were suddenly bathed in shadows and a peach-tinted glow. A lullaby began to play softly in the background.

They smiled at each other, the tinkling melody no longer keeping them estranged but joined, as they should be.

Once the song had played twice, Myles shut off the music-box control.

"Sweet," he said. "But not the kind of music I had in mind."

"Good. At the moment I'd rather be a woman than a mother. Though, Myles . . ."

"Hmmm?" he murmured, nuzzling her neck.

"What I said about almost wishing it wasn't yours . . . nothing could be farther from the truth. I'm thrilled I'm having your baby."

"And not the other man's?" Jealousy nipped at his heels again, tightening his chest with the need to possess her. And he would.

Faith hesitated, studying his face. She seemed to want to say something, something important.

"What?" he said. "I'm being ridiculous. I have no right to those years or the feelings you had for someone else. But no matter how hard I try, I can't seem to get past it. You bring out something in me that makes me hate the thought of sharing you with another man, even a mystery man buried in your past."

"You're the only man who matters to me, Myles. No one ever mattered to me the way you do."

"In that case I'll put my jealousy aside." He slid her down his length and plucked the few pins left in her hair. "And get on with finishing what we started earlier."

Her cheeks were flushed with anticipation, but she looked away, suddenly shy.

"I'm nervous," she admitted with a small laugh.

"Then I'll have to put you at ease, won't I? Let's see," he murmured as he kneeled and removed a gold pump. "First the shoes." He lifted her other foot and kissed it before sliding the heel off. "You'll dance much easier without these."

His palms moved up her calves, then drew slow, intricate circles around her knees. He could feel a fine tremble in response to his light touch.

"And I'll want to feel your bare skin while we move, so you don't mind if I take this off, too, do you, dear?" He didn't wait for permission but glided his hands upward over the cool silk of her hose, feeling the warmth of her flesh beneath.

He was aching. He'd been aching all night, all month, and maybe even for years, only he'd refused to acknowledge its existence. The hunger was too great, and he was bent on taking her slowly, not trusting himself to unleash the force of passion that was already gnawing at his resolve.

He hooked his fingers into her hose and panties

and peeled them down, feeling her shake. Feeling himself begin to shake.

Once they were off, he rose and stared at her face, tilted backward, eyes closed, lips parted.

"Now we dance," he whispered roughly.

"I already hear the music," she murmured, and swayed into him.

A groan caught in his throat. His teeth clenched while his body demanded that he take her immediately. Furiously. Without gentle persuasion or time to savor.

"This is just the intro. I think we need some lyrics to make it last." He forced himself to go to the sound system they'd set up after unpacking. The disks in the CD player were familiar to him; they held sensual, fluid music, perfect for a night of erotic discovery.

He pressed a button.

Sound filtered through the room, weaving its magic web as he took her in his arms. Her own lifted, and he felt one hand brush over the back of his neck while the other sifted through his hair. Her nails against his scalp caused him to shiver, and he pulled her closer as he imagined them sinking into his back.

They danced easily, naturally, with motions that suggested they'd been partners for a very long while. His hand moved over the lamé covering her back, and he pulled the zipper down. As smooth as a whisper, it obliged him and parted, giving him access to her bare back.

He fanned his fingers over the smoothness of her skin, exploring it until she moaned and began to release the buttons of his shirt. Quickly he shrugged it off, then drew down the bodice of her dress. They danced, bare-chested, rubbing lightly against each other until he could feel the tautness of her nipples brushing against him. Her sighs of arousal were more delicious and heady than the strains of music.

He bent her back just far enough to nip and suckle her until she cried for more.

"I'll give you more," he promised, then tensed as his unruly body demanded he stop the play and take and take and take without regard to her condition. "There's a problem, though. I might be more than you bargained for."

"Never. I want too much. I want it all."

He inhaled the feminine scent from her neck, her wrists, her hair.

"Torture," he murmured, sipping at her lips. "The sweetest torture I've ever endured. I want you to pay for making me suffer."

"Gladly," she answered. "Take any price you want."

"I won't be fair," he warned, his heart pounding too hard and fast. His control unraveled to a slender thread as he lifted her up and rubbed the moisture from her breasts on his chest. "I'll make you cry for me. And when you do, I won't be able to stop. Even if you ask for mercy."

"I don't want mercy. I want you. Take me to bed, Myles. Enough."

He turned her until her back was against him and her buttocks pressed intimately against his groin. He lifted her dress, grasping her, learning how lovely she was made, touching her however he wanted. If she was shocked, she didn't protest.

He ground against her, no longer able to think as he struggled with his raging passion. He was so dangerously close to losing the battle.

But he loved her enough not to give in.

He played with the hair guarding her feminine heat, hearing her rasping breath, feeling the springy texture that was moist. He couldn't stop himself from imagining how she might taste . . .

Her legs nearly buckled. "I can't wait . . . Let the dance be over. It's time, Myles. Past time."

She rubbed frantically against him, shameless in her own want. A hoarse groan tore from his throat. He turned her around, clenching her tight.

"Oh, God, Faith. You don't know. It's tearing at me, it's been building for so long. I haven't hardly touched you and I'm half out of my mind wanting to drive into you as hard and fast as I can." Staring into her eyes, he saw the urgency of her need. "Don't you understand? I'm afraid of hurting you."

"You won't hurt me. The doctor said—"

"In this case the doctor could be wrong."

"She wouldn't have given us permission if she'd had any doubts."

"But *I* have doubts." He grasped her behind and rubbed between the cradle of her thighs. "Faith, you have to listen to me. *I . . . have . . . no . . . control.*"

The starkness of his primitive need bore into her consciousness. She wanted Myles this way, driven by a desire that could shake even a man like him with its force. Shutting her mind to the tiny voice of apprehension, she insinuated her hand between their meshed bodies and kneaded the rigid flesh straining against his fly.

He continued to look at her through slitted eyes, breathing in harsh gasps.

"I want this to last."

"There'll be other times." She found his buckle with her other hand and began to undo it.

"I want to see you naked. I want . . . I want to see what I've only felt."

"You can," she whispered, her fingers curving over the shape of him. "Soon, Myles. Soon . . ."

"I've imagined kissing you there, tasting you."

"You don't have to imagine anymore. It's yours, yours for the taking." The sound of his zipper rasping open mingled with their choppy breathing.

"Oh, God," he groaned, his head falling back, his face taut with agony.

Their fevered hands shed the remains of each other's clothes. There wasn't time to admire his physique. He was a blur of rough hair, hard muscle, and tensing strength. Myles pulled her along the short distance to the bed, touching her wherever he could as they frantically rubbed and grappled, nearly stumbling in their haste.

He tumbled her down and stretched out over her, his hardness pressing against her belly.

"I didn't want the first time to be like this," he rasped. "But there's no other way."

"We make our own way." She couldn't control the shivering of her body or her questing hand from reaching for him.

He caught her wrist in a steely grip.

"Later," he growled in warning. "For now, just trust me. Do what I say, and we'll be all right."

"Tell me what to do. I don't know what you want."

"This . . ." he answered.

He slid back and forth against her, pretending it was enough.

"It's not enough," she whimpered, straining toward him.

"It *has* to be," he insisted. He ground his mouth over hers, letting his tongue glide rapidly and mate with hers in a way he could not.

"No. Inside," she pleaded. "When you're inside."

"Not this time." He began to move more frantically, allowing the contact to deepen just a fraction.

He was only making her ache worse, and she could have wept with his refusal. She arched, opening her thighs wider, silently begging for more.

"We do it this way," he groaned between a plea and a command. "Next time, next . . . time. When I have some kind of control."

"Damn you," she cried. "Damn you for doing this to me, leaving me hurting like this. It's not enough, not half enough." She locked her legs around his hips, tilting upward. "Can't you feel my body crying? Can't you feel me shake? Take me, *all* of me. Lose your damnable control."

With an anguished groan, he grasped her hips, his fingers biting into her skin. He took the weight of his belly off hers while his head dropped forward and he stared down at her with a glittering fury that was wild and consuming.

As she waited for a moment that was an eternity, she smelled the mingled sweat sheening their torsos. A salty drop fell from his brow onto her upper lip, and she licked it, savoring the liquid of his body with her tongue. His face was harsh, intense. Beloved. The hair covering his legs was rough against hers, and she embraced the slight discomfort with gladness, knowing each of these things would be seared into her memory to cherish for a lifetime.

He thrust into her with a powerful jerk of his hips, sinking into her until she had taken him fully.

She was so ready, so eager to embrace him as hers and hers alone that she welcomed even the pain in her tender flesh. Then she felt her body adjust to the unfamiliar fullness of him inside her.

He moved over her, whispering, "Mine . . . all mine. You belong to me."

"I've always belonged to you," she answered while tears trickled down the side of her face at the wonder of his possession, their union.

She moved against him, marveling at the pleasure that flooded through her.

"Dance," she told him. "Dance like you've never danced before."

He obeyed with a tempo that was demanding, desperate, beyond imagination. She was no match for him, and when she could no longer meet the demand of his body, she gave herself into his keeping and let him take control.

She didn't want it to end. She fought against the tide trying to take her away, out of herself and into a dark universe sparked only by his forceful grind, his chest sweetly punishing her breasts. His growls mingled with her own murmurings, lacing in words that were inarticulate and had no meaning other than greed and love and need.

The tide broke. She climaxed with a ripping force that came in wave upon wave of shimmering, unearthly sensation. She sobbed his name, and he echoed hers before he crushed her lips with his and invaded her mouth to seek and receive a fierce, savage kiss. Then there was the flood, the hot liquid of his body emptying itself, and hers absorbing the seed he planted.

Their bodies continued to shudder as if chilled to the bone though their skin was fevered, hot to the touch. Against their joined lips Myles was groaning her name over and over. His hands moved to her hair and began to stroke, to soothe, as he rubbed his cheek against her tear-stained one.

"You're crying," he said, anxiety threading his rough voice. Raising his face quickly, he searched her eyes for any sign of distress. "Did I hurt you?" he demanded. "Tell me. Now."

"No, no. I'm just crying because I'm so . . . happy." She sighed in contentment as lethargy settled into her muscles. Realizing her nails were digging into his back, she abruptly released him and cupped his face, the light beard rubbing against her palms. "Did I hurt you?" she asked anxiously.

"Oh, yes, you did," he murmured intimately, running his lips over a ruby-painted nail before nipping a finger. "You hurt me so good."

As if his words whispered a reminder to her body, she began to feel a little of the discomfort she'd escaped during the heat of the moment. Faith winced before she could tell herself not to.

"I'm heavy. As much as I hate to do this . . ." He began to roll off her. Faith quickly grabbed him.

"I don't want you to leave," she insisted while her mind came fully awake. If she didn't do something quick, she was going to have a lot of explaining to do. "Let's turn off the light and snuggle," she suggested, hugging him close with one arm while reaching for the light with the other.

"Better yet, let's leave on the light and snuggle." Myles caught her hand at the lamp switch. "I want to look you over. Just to make sure I left you all in one piece."

"Look tomorrow," she said quickly, fighting her rising sense of urgency. She reached for the lamp again, and he grabbed her wrist, beginning to frown.

"What don't you want me to see?" he demanded.

"Nothing!" She forced her voice to remain calm. "Nothing. I'm just tired, that's all."

"If that's all, then you won't mind resting while I put my mind at ease, will you?"

He got off her, and when she quickly reached for the light, he manacled her wrists with a single hand while his other began tracing the length of her body.

His brow was furrowed in concentration as he

slid his fingertips over her breasts, then lower to her abdomen, carefully examining her. As he began to move lower, she struggled.

"No, Myles," she entreated. "Don't."

She moaned, trying vainly to twist away from his stern grip. What would she say? How could she explain without giving herself away? And why was she beginning to respond to his inquiring touch, the vague pain giving way to a far deeper ache?

And then he wasn't feeling her anymore. He was touching and staring at the sheet in disbelief and groaning, "My God, of my God . . . I'll never forgive myself."

He abruptly released her and bounded off the bed, heading straight for the phone beside the sound system where the music continued to play.

She went after him, and he barked an order for her to stay put. As he frantically began to punch out a number, Faith reached him and depressed the button in the telephone's cradle.

"What the—get back in bed. I'm calling the doctor."

"Myles, it's not what you think."

He held out his hand, slightly tinged with her blood and rasped, "Not what I think? Faith, I—"

"Took my virginity."

For a full minute he stared at her mutely, stunned.

"I did *what*?"

"Please, Myles, come back to bed."

"Why didn't you tell me?" he demanded, beginning to look not only shocked but enormously relieved.

"Because . . ." Her legs began to shake, and he caught her to him, holding her close, feathering possessive kisses on her temple. "Because I was afraid you wouldn't go to bed with me if you knew. Or you'd think . . . there was something wrong with me. I thought it might bother you."

"Bother me? What are you, nuts? I'm ecstatic, I'm thrilled, I'm"—he held her away, shaking his head—"confused. I'm amazed, and wondering what the hell kept you waiting this long. You're not what I'd call timid. And you didn't exactly seem inexperienced."

"I'm not inexperienced. Just not, umm . . . deflowered."

"What were you waiting for?" He studied her closely.

"The right man." That much was true.

"Weren't you ever curious? For a modern woman, you're not keeping up with the times."

"Sure I was curious, and I certainly satisfied my curiosity to a point. Far enough to be disappointed when the fireworks I expected never came." She wouldn't mention how each Christmas vacation, each summer visit with him and Gloria had stoked her ceaseless longing and sabotaged any relationship that was close to intimacy. "I'm no prude," she added, "but I was stubborn enough to hold out for a memorable experience."

"Stubborn, huh? For some reason I don't have too much trouble buying that."

She punched him playfully, then ran her hands over his chest before softly biting into the firmness of muscle.

"It was worth the wait," she assured him.

Myles chuckled. "And here I was eaten up with jealousy because another man had taken my woman first."

"You're the first, Myles," she whispered, letting her eyes tell him all the things she couldn't yet share. It was too soon; what would he think if he knew she had coveted her own sister's husband, especially after their bitter confrontation over the pictures?

"The first," he concurred, gently picking her up and striding purposefully toward the bed. "And the last."

Eleven

"Good morning, Mrs. Wellington. Or maybe I should say, good afternoon, sleepyhead."

Faith's answer was a muted groan, and her left hand groped for the covers he'd moved away from her back. He smiled as the diamond wedding ring on her finger winked a two-carat greeting.

Myles traced a path of kisses down the curve of spine turned to him. Faith had given up sleeping on her stomach over a month ago, due to the baby's spurt of growth. Thank goodness they only had two months to go. He didn't mind being woken up by a strong, unexpected kick from her belly in the middle of the night, or by Faith tossing incessantly in their big new bed as she tried to get comfortable. But he missed their fiery, passionate interludes. They slept naked, made love gently, frequently, but even that was proving to be a test of his mettle.

Still, the love that remained unspoken for his

wife and the child she carried for him curbed the hungry urgency eating at his control. No, he hadn't told her in words how much he loved her, but his actions spoke for him. He put aside his more demanding needs; he ignored her mood swings; he tramped through pouring rain for take-out Chinese when he really wanted a drink, his wife, and a warm bed after a long, hard day at work. Did she love him too? He thought so, even if she did seem more preoccupied with her pregnancy than with him half the time.

Myles frowned, displeased. Jealousy again. Just when he'd gotten over the mystery man, he'd begun to wrestle with a surprising and ridiculous resentment over the baby's demands on his wife's emotions and body. It wasn't a very flattering realization, and he struggled to rise above this maddening possessiveness.

"It's Saturday," she grumbled, though she arched against his mouth with a gratifying moan, and her searching fingers forgot about the covers and trailed through his hair. "I want to spend the day in bed."

Myles stretched behind her, fitting their bodies together like two spoons.

Nuzzling against her neck, he chuckled. "Sounds good to me, but I think Carol's expecting to see the wedding pictures, not the two of us cavorting in the sack. She'll be here in an hour, and you haven't eaten breakfast—or rather, lunch—yet."

"Not hungry," she muttered. "Besides, I'll just get indigestion."

"Maybe what I've got in mind for a snack isn't usually served on a tray or the table."

Faith giggled in a low, throaty voice, and he could feel a surge of response in his groin.

She rolled over and looked at him with dreamy, sleep-filled eyes.

"Two's company," she said, "but the crowd"—she patted her belly—"is putting in an appearance before Carol gets here."

"The crowd seems to forget that two months of marriage means we're still on our honeymoon." Myles gulped down a grimace; he loved this baby almost as much as he loved Faith, but the intrusions were becoming more frequent and were doing nothing to appease his masculine appetite. "I'm warning you, wife. Once the company's in its crib, your husband's got plans to make up for lost time."

"What kind of plans?" Her lips tilted upward, into a coy come-on. "I'd like to hear them, each and every naughty one."

"Shockingly naughty," he assured her. He whispered a graphic scenario into her ears, wanting more than anything to put his words into action.

"Myles!" she gasped. "That's . . . that's—"

"Decadent? Risqué?"

"Indecent and . . . very creative."

"Do I take that to mean you'd indulge me?"

"But what if my figure's not as . . . appealing as it was before I got pregnant? I might be a disappointment. I do have a few stretch marks."

"Those are marks you should be proud of, Faith.

I treasure them. And besides, you'll always be beautiful to me, perfect or not."

She snuggled in closer and purred, "In that case I'll indulge you in anything. You're my husband." She gave his title the sound of a loving caress. "I married you, wickedness and all."

"You did that," he murmured, kissing the ring on her finger. "But I was never that wicked until you came along. You're a witchy woman, Faith Wellington, bringing out the beast in me. It's a liberating feeling to know I can growl anything I like, even if it's impure, and you're still there. Accepting me just as I am."

"More than accept, Myles."

Loving me?

"Wanting you," she said. "Wanting to spend my life with you."

Myles hesitated. Faith had a right to know. Even if it was a truth he didn't want to accept himself, one that was dark and had inflicted more than a little pain in his growing years, it was time to come clean with his wife.

"Even though I'm a bastard?"

"A bastard?" she repeated. "Where did that come from? You're not—"

"I am." He leaned over her, letting her see the deeply imbedded thorn that could still pierce his soul. "I should have told you before now, but . . . my pride got in the way. My mother didn't die when I was young, that's just the story I led everyone to believe. She was, shall we say, a lady of the night who got knocked up by my father.

Or at least she was a good enough actress to make him believe I was his. Once he was stuck with the goods, she disappeared."

"Oh, Myles," she whispered, reaching up to stroke the stern lines of his face. "How horrible for you."

He looked away, remembering, confronting the bitterness still inside him. "I'll never forget the night I found out. I was seven, and my father was drunk, stewing over bills and griping about having an extra mouth to feed. That's when he let it slip, along with his suspicion I wasn't even his kid. He was sober the next day and tried to apologize."

Myles's laugh was short, harsh. "He wasn't very good at saying he was sorry. Maybe I was his after all. It's not too easy for me to humble myself either. Our relationship was never quite the same after that. Even as I aged and could understand a man's resentment for having to raise a child that possibly belonged to some nameless stranger, there was always this . . . distance."

"I'm so sorry, Myles, when I called you a— If only I'd known."

"Few people do. It's something I grew up abhorring. I even misled . . . Gloria." Her name was still dear, her memory cherished, but the reality of their life together had receded to a sweet, distant dream. The present was so real, his marriage to Faith pulsing, fulfilling, exciting. "I'm not too proud of myself for that deceit. She deserved the truth. But I've always been ashamed of the one thing I could never change. Even after all these years

I feel a little tainted. But there it is, and maybe now you can understand why I was so determined to save my child from the same stigma."

"It was a reflex and I can't blame you for that. I do understand, Myles. Much better than I did before."

Her acceptance was a healing balm to his old wound. Now that he had finally taken the leap, he wanted to tell her all. "I vowed to myself a long time ago that I'd carve out a legacy for my children, begin traditions that started with me, since my own parentage isn't really certain. Maybe that's why having a family of my own means so much to me."

"Why didn't you tell me that to begin with? I would have married you in Denver and in name only if I'd known."

"Why? I didn't want you to feel sorry for me. I can take your anger, Faith, but never your pity. It's too much of an affront to my pride. And once you were here, it didn't take long for me to realize giving you my name wouldn't be nearly enough."

She slid her hands into his hair, urging his mouth to come a whisper away from hers.

"You once said having to prove you're strong all the time is a weakness in itself. I think this just proves your point. You're the most virile man I've ever known, Myles Wellington. Physically, yes, but in every other way too. I could never pity you. Just as I couldn't bear your keeping such a sensitive part of your life shuttered away from me. I want all of you. Every thought. Every emotion." She traced his lips with the tip of her tongue. "Every fantasy."

They met, mouth-to-mouth. He poured all his

bitterness and need and liberated release into the urgency of their healing kiss.

Faith undid his pants as they kissed, stroking him, charging him with familiar passion. He rolled her to her side and entered her from behind, their hips moving in perfect sync. His hands glided over her, knowing exactly how to please her, caressing just the right places to bring her to the peak.

He poured himself into her, giving up the last remnants of his childhood exile with a groan that rolled up from the hidden places of his soul.

He exulted in the instinctive knowledge that she cherished even his darkness, and he emerged with a feeling that was wondrous and new.

"And this is Jennifer, my best friend, from Denver, who was my maid of honor." Faith handed the glossy to Carol to add to the growing stack. "A friend of Myles's took the pictures. We liked the idea of having the personal touch. It seemed appropriate, since it was such a small wedding."

"Small but beautiful," Carol said with approval. "I'm so sentimental, I could practically cry just looking at these. Larry's always embarrassed to go to weddings with me. I even got teary-eyed watching Charles and Di on TV."

Looking away from Carol, who continued to pour over the photos, Faith smiled at Myles sitting beside her. The small space between them filled up with unspoken words, a remembered tenderness that was treasured, and a sense of shared trust.

Soon she would show him the sculpture. It was between them, though he didn't know it, the one secret she withheld. When the time was right, she would tell him all. What held her back, she wasn't sure. Perhaps it was the baby. Perhaps it was not knowing exactly how Myles might take the news. Or maybe she was just waiting to hear him say three magic words. Whatever the reason was, her instincts insisted that the perfect moment would present itself. Today hadn't been it. The invulnerable man had been vulnerable to her; confessing her own hidden hurts would have to wait.

"How many people did you have?" Carol asked.

"Ten," Myles answered, draping his arm around Faith's shoulders. "All close friends."

"No family?"

His arm tensed.

"No," Faith interjected quickly. "Myles's parents passed away some time ago. Mine have been gone since I was eighteen. After they went down in a small plane, Gloria and I stuck together. She was always the steady one, as much mother to me as sister." Staring at the pictures, Faith again experienced the odd sensation that had gripped her at the wedding. Shaking it off, she added, "We missed my cousin Martin at the ceremony. He's in Europe on business."

"I keep wondering what it is he says he has for us," Myles mused. "He was so cryptic."

"By the way," Faith said, "did we mention that our Lamaze classes start next week?"

"How exciting! I wish they'd had such things when Larry and I were having our babies. We have five kids, which wasn't so out of the ordinary then. Nowadays, though, people seem to stop at one or two."

Myles and Faith exchanged knowing glances. Carol was nothing if not consistent.

"I don't think ours is destined to be an only child," Faith ventured, realizing they hadn't discussed the possibility of more. Their marriage was still new.

"Once we hit an even dozen, we might decide we've got enough," Myles put in with a chuckle, winking broadly at Faith.

Surely he wasn't serious. This pregnancy seemed to be lasting forever; how many times would she be willing to go through this, to relinquish herself for a new life? And how many demands would a child put on their relationship? How much time would she have for the career she'd worked so hard to build? As it was, she couldn't keep up.

As Carol bid them good-bye and good luck, Faith stared after her, the questions tumbling like so many dice.

"What's wrong, sweetheart?" Myles put his arms around her, but she pulled away slightly.

"You don't really want a dozen children, do you?"

"I used to think I did. And you know how much our own family means to me." He gazed down at her thoughtfully, a frown creasing his brow. "I have to admit that lately, though, I've started getting selfish about not wanting to share you. But I'm coming to terms with it . . . sort of. I keep telling myself that mature, grown men don't try hoarding their wives away from their own children."

Faith bit her lower lip. "Mature, grown women do. At least this one does."

"You too?"

She gazed at him anxiously. "Does that mean we're horrible, Myles? That we won't be good parents?"

"No. I think it means we're sharing some of the same anxieties over a lot of unknowns. I like to think it means we've got a strong enough marriage to confess what we wouldn't to anyone else and that we're bringing our child into a home full of trust and . . . love." He smiled ruefully and added, "I do feel a lot less guilty now. I'm thinking I'm only human instead of a selfish ogre."

"You haven't had the corner on that market. I've been thinking . . . or maybe trying not to think lately about . . ." Faith eyed him levelly. "Myles, what about my career?"

"What about it? Do you want to cut back some more? Or better yet, quit the accounts you've got left and come work for me. The benefits are terrific, pay's not bad, work the hours you want, and you can sleep your way to the top."

"Stop joking, Myles. I'm serious about this."

"So am I. If past experience is any indicator, we make a damn good team." He pulled her against him, ruthless in his attempts at persuasion. "I have a lot of respect for what you do. I'd never ask you to give up something I wouldn't be willing to give up myself . . . but I could be totally unscrupulous when it comes to keeping you as close to me as I can."

"I'm a hard sell," she warned, even as she warmed to the idea. "You'd better throw your best pitch."

"Okay. For starters I don't like you working late the way you do some nights when I can see you're ready to drop. I sit on my hands to keep from yanking you away from your drafting table."

"I . . . suspected as much. One of free-lancing's drawbacks. You don't like my deadlines, do you?"

"The only time I resent your work is when it eats into our time together. That's why I think we'd both be happier if you closed shop here and put your time in at my office. Besides, it would give us a chance to work on projects away from home and baby. Sure, that part of our lives is the most important, but it's healthy to have more in common than just that and to keep from getting so caught up with our separate careers that we catch quickies and conversation on the fly while we try to raise a family."

Faith thought of the nights she'd already spent working during their marriage and of the mornings she'd woken up to an empty bed. She thought of the women she knew who loved their husbands but didn't seem to know them anymore, the demands of family and job slowly driving them apart, making them near strangers.

"Okay, you've got my attention. Let's hear the plan," she finally said.

"You close your ears and eyes to the weeping and gnashing of teeth when you break the news to your clients. Wind up what you've got, take as much maternity leave as you want, and when you're ready to start working again, pick the days and hours you want."

"But who'll take care of the baby?"

"Simple. We'll hire a part-time nanny. If you're still nursing when you decide to come back to work, I'll have a nursery put in the office so that she and the baby can be handy. I've been planning to get one started for the other women at work anyway."

"What if we disagree, as we're bound to?"

"As long as you don't undermine my authority at work, you can disagree as much as you like. We respect each other professionally. If it gets too personal, we'll just have to work out our differences of opinion in private."

"The other employees might resent me. You wouldn't exactly be unprejudiced."

"Smart people don't bite the hand that feeds them. Besides, once they get a load of your work, they'll be thanking me for bringing you in."

Faith considered him and his suggestions one by one. "Why do I get the feeling that this isn't off-the-cuff?"

"Because it isn't off-the-cuff. I've been plotting this whole scheme since before we got married."

"You're manipulating me. Pulling all the right strings."

Myles slid his hand up her maternity top to fondle a breast.

"I should hope so. But maybe a little more

practice would help. Tell me which string makes you weaker."

Faith moaned her assent as he found her weakest string.

"Enough," she finally pleaded. "I give up. We win."

He sealed the victory with a heart-stopping kiss. The baby stamped its approval with yet another kick.

"Oh, that was hard!" She jumped as a flurry of activity commenced. "And . . . oh no, the hiccups again."

Myles grinned broadly as he stared down at her belly.

"Looks like one hell of a party in there. Junior must have had too much to drink."

They laughed, and it felt so good, so right. Myles pressed his hand over her belly; she pressed her own over his.

"You know who I miss, Myles?"

"I miss her too, Faith."

"As strange as it sounds . . . at the wedding, of all the people I wished were there . . ."

"Gloria," he whispered.

"Yes. I missed her worse than ever then. And only you can understand how I felt."

"She was there," he murmured, pressing his lips to her temple. "I felt her there."

"I feel her now," Faith whispered.

"So do I." Myles stroked his hand over her belly as it quieted. "And she's smiling."

Twelve

"Hey, gorgeous, are you almost ready to go? We don't want to be late for our last session."

Faith didn't answer. She stared down morosely at her untied laces. Her back hurt. She could hardly breathe. And she was carrying so much baby she didn't seem to have room for food or drink. Though that wasn't true, judging from the number of her trips to the bathroom. The August heat didn't help her hot flashes either, even with the thermostat set near freezing.

"I don't want to go," she muttered crossly. "I want to stay home and be miserable."

She glanced up at Myles, who stood in the doorway, looking maddeningly calm and comfortable in the jeans hugging his well-built hips. That was another thing—she was so sick of maternity clothes, she could scream. She felt like a beached whale and thought she looked like one. She couldn't even get out of bed or a low-slung chair without a hand.

"You go on," she said irritably. "I'll stay."

"Are you crazy? You're due in two weeks. Every time my pager goes off, I have palpitations. Every time you groan or try to get out of bed, I'm ready to jump into my pants and fly out the door."

"At least you can get into them," she accused. "Go away. I want to be alone."

"What's wrong, Garbo?" He smiled tenderly and came to kneel beside her chair. "I won't leave you alone until you tell me."

She was being unreasonable and she knew it, but dammit, how could he understand? How could anyone understand, unless that person had been eight and a half months pregnant?

Suddenly so tired of it all—the pregnancy, the fatigue, the horrible discomfort—she gave in to the need to cry, to get something out of her system, even if it wasn't what was kicking her under the ribs.

"I can't tie my shoes," she sobbed.

Myles put his arms around her and drew her close, as close as her stomach allowed. It became hard, tensing up until it felt like a major-league bowling ball. The Braxton-Hicks contractions, preparing her body for the real event, had been on the rise lately, but this one was worse than most.

"There . . . there now," he soothed, kissing away her tears and pushing back the tangle of her hair. "I'll tie them for you. See? They're done. Now, why don't I help you up and we'll go see our friends. They'll miss you, even if you are the prettiest one there, and you'll feel better if you see some other pregnant women. At least they're as miserable as you."

"I wish you wouldn't be so nice. It makes me feel bad, and I feel bad enough as it is."

"I know you do. I'd have the baby for you if I could."

She sniffled and held tight to her husband. Knowing that he would do anything possible to ease her discomfort, even the pain to come. It gave her the fortitude to put her depression aside and try to make the best of the night. Myles was right. She would feel better after seeing their new friends, friends from all walks of life who shared in the excitement and intensity of becoming parents soon. They would do their exercises—again—they would visit and then go to the nursery window in the hospital where the classes were held and dream of seeing their baby there soon.

"Okay." She swiped at her nose and the few remaining tears, then summoned a halfhearted smile. "Help me up and we'll go."

"That's my girl. Hang in there, sweet. It won't be long. And just remember, I'm with you all the way."

With a practiced motion Myles fitted his arms beneath hers and lifted. Faith stood, teetering as she gained her balance. She tried to remember what it was like when she'd sauntered around on highheels with a self-assured sway of the hips. It seemed so long ago; now she waddled like a duck.

Myles tucked an arm around her waist and helped her down the stairs and to the mini-van they'd bought. Just as she put a foot on the running board, she tensed.

He knew from experience that she was having a Braxton-Hicks contraction and quickly whipped out his stopwatch. This one seemed harder and was lasting longer.

"We'll get a head start on the class with our practice. Breathe with me now. Deep breath . . . let it out slow . . . and inhale—"

"Put it away," she growled, impatient with the techniques they practiced ad nauseum each night. "Just put the damn stopwatch away while I—*Oh!*"

Warm water gushed between her thighs, streaming down her legs into her shoes, thoroughly soaking her pants.

"Myles! My water! It—"

"*Ohmygod!* Oh, no, stay calm . . . stay . . . what do I do? Go to the hospital . . . call the doctor . . . pack your bags—"

"Myles, get a grip. I packed two weeks ago, remember?"

Faith struggled with the impulse to laugh hysterically at the sight of her controlled husband going into a tizzy.

"Packed, right. The bags, the bags. I'll get the bags."

He automatically pivoted, ready to head for the house.

"Myles! Don't leave me here! I'm completely wet. Help me inside so that I can at least change my clothes."

"No! Get in the car. We're leaving right now."

"I can't get in the car. The seat will get wet."

"The hell with the seat. We're having a baby!"

Faith resisted as he tried to urge her inside.

"We're not having a baby until you get my bags and something for me to sit on. I'll wait here while you go back and—"

She almost doubled over with another gripping contraction, latching onto Myles and digging her fingers into his arm.

Myles started breathing with her as if on automatic pilot. Once the contraction was over, he gathered his wits, ready to assume his role of coach and husband and father.

"Okay, Faith. This is what we do. You get in and don't say another word about the seats. This is our baby and I'll keep this car till the day I die because its water is on it. I'm going inside and calling the hospital to let them know we're on our way. While they call Dr. Laurentz, I'll get those bags you want, and than we're gone." He kissed her in reassurance, and in the dim light his eyes willed his support to her, his belief in her courage. "Can you handle five minutes alone?"

She nodded, and he quickly helped her up. Handing her the stopwatch, he instructed, "Keep this. If you have another one, time it." Seconds later when he was already inside the house, she felt the beginnings of another contraction.

"Please, God," she whispered. "Please let me be strong. I'm hurting and I'm scared."

She rose to the challenge of another contraction; only it was harder, longer, fierce. Nothing was as she'd imagined it. Her first birthing was supposed to start slow and give her a chance to get ready. It could take hours . . . *hours!* How could she endure it?

A vision of Myles gave her the answer. For him she would endure anything, even this terrible pain she had never imagined possible. She focused on him, she focused on the baby, the moment they would claim it in their arms. . . .

"They're expecting us," Myles said excitedly, throwing her luggage into the seat behind them and slamming the door shut. "Did you have another one?"

"I'll say," she said, dreading the next one. He revved the engine. Faith grabbed his hand. "Don't leave me," she said urgently as her stomach began to knot up. "Please don't leave me again."

He returned the pressure of her grip. "I'll never leave you. I love you."

"Myles," she whispered, tears gathering again, of joy then the pain this time, "I lo—ah!"

He helped her through it, then immediately shifted the van into gear. Like a man possessed, he drove through the thin traffic, following the route they'd mapped out before. Faith noticed a flashing red light coming up close behind them, but Myles was oblivious to the siren's sound.

When he didn't pull over, the police car drove up to race alongside them. A horn honked, and the officer gestured.

Myles rolled down his window. "We're having a baby!" he yelled.

Whether the officer could read lips or was able to see her doubling over, she wasn't sure. But he quickly nodded and with a grin signaled for them to follow him. He zipped in front and led the way, giving them an impressive escort right to the emergency-room entrance.

"I told you I had clout," Myles said with a chuckle as he quickly helped Faith from the van. The policeman hopped out to ask if he could be of further assistance.

"Thanks, officer. You've done plenty," Myles assured him, fumbling with their bags and managing to give the man a business card at the same time. Faith concentrated on puffing and panting. "Give me a call and I'll be sure to give you an extra good deal. Along with a cigar."

An orderly appeared with a wheelchair, and before Faith could blink, she was being raced inside. Everything happened so fast, she didn't have time to think. There was the quick change to a gown, a prep, an I.V., and electrodes to monitor the baby. Sandwiched between all this, a nurse measured her dilation, then quickly ran back to the birthing ward's station. Myles disappeared just long enough to throw on a surgical gown.

"Myles!" she cried, grasping his hand when he returned. "Don't leave me again. You said you wouldn't leave—"

"Oh, baby, I'm sorry." He winced as her nails dug into his hand. "How bad is—breathe . . . pant, pant—"

"Shut up!"

Myles's startled and uncomprehending gaze swung to the composed face of Dr. Laurentz, who was garbed in sterile hospital green.

"Don't worry," she whispered. "She doesn't really

know what she's saying. She's striking out at the pain, not you."

"Give her something. Don't let her hurt anymore," he pleaded. "I can't stand it."

"Too late. She was dilated eight centimeters when the nurse measured her ten minutes ago. We're already going into the final stretch, and a shot or an epidural would only prolong her labor. I've seen more births than I can count, but your wife's coming faster than any first baby I've seen." She patted Myles's free hand while his other stroked a wet cloth over Faith's fevered brow.

"But what can I do? Tell me. Anything and I'll do it."

"You already are." She nodded at the gentle way he tended his wife. "Don't worry. You're doing great. Just keep reminding her the baby's almost here." Leaning down, she said firmly, "Faith, can you hear me?"

Her head thrashing against the white pillow, she fought the pain engulfing her body. Why were they bothering her? When would it end? The pressure . . . the pressure bearing down . . .

"I have to push!" she screamed.

"Don't push," Dr. Laurentz ordered sternly. "Wait until I give you the okay."

"*I have to push,*" she urgently insisted. "Oh God, I have to—"

"Now I need you," the doctor said to Myles. "While I'm measuring, you get in her face and make her pant. She'll listen to you before she will me." Slapping on a pair of thin plastic gloves, she turned to the nurse hovering close by. "Get the other nurses. Make sure the anesthesiologist is around, just in case. Call the nursery to get that incubator here pronto and make sure the delivery tray's ready."

Myles turned his back to the frenzied activity. "Faith, don't push, please."

She swiped at him, and he grabbed her hands. "Listen to me," he ordered. "You *can't* push."

Even though his face was mere inches from hers, she had trouble focusing. Myles wasn't making any sense. Not push? How could she not push when the pressure was so immense, demanding she bear down with all her might?

"I . . . can't . . . stop. . . ." she groaned between clenched teeth.

"You can. I know you can. Just hold tight to me and pant . . . pant!"

She did hold tight, squeezing the circulation out of his hands. She tried to concentrate on his face, blocking out everything but him and doing her best to imitate his rapid, shallow pants. Myles was her rock, her one link left in the world. She clung to the strength he offered. Myles would keep her safe. Myles would take care of her and make everything all right. He loved her. He would never leave her.

"Great news!" Dr. Laurentz motioned the nurses to set up the bed for delivery and position a mirror so that the parents could watch their child emerge. "Not only are you fully dilated, but your baby's close to crowning. I can see hair. Lots of it!"

"Did you hear that, sweetheart? Our baby has hair!"

"Hair?" she whispered. "Our baby's so close?"

"Yes," Myles assured her in a choked voice. "Look at the foot of the bed. You can even see the top of the head in the mirror."

She stared down in wonder at the tiny bit of life she had carried inside her body, a person created from her union with the man she loved more than ever in this moment of pain and glory.

"Can I push?" she asked anxiously.

"Next contraction, Faith." Dr. Laurentz positioned herself on a stool and accepted an instrument. "First I have to make sure you don't tear. Look at Myles while I do this and you won't feel a thing. Believe it or not, I deadened you while you were busy with your husband. All that pressure you've been feeling actually helps me out. Nature knows what she's doing. I'm just assisting."

Faith stared up at Myles, her eyes filling with tears while the excitement of it all lifted her soul to heights unknown.

"Lift her up, Myles. And Faith, you push. Push like your life depends on it."

She did, the sensation of relief near ecstasy. Myles cheered her on, and she pushed even harder. It became a ritual of push . . . relax . . . push. . . . Time lost all meaning as they worked together.

Suddenly Dr. Laurentz called out, "The head is coming. Push hard!"

"Push . . . push . . . *Push!*" All the nurses chanted, with Myles's voice overriding theirs.

With a magnificent growl that ripped from her throat, Faith bore down with renewed strength.

"Stop!" shouted the doctor. "Just a small push

and . . . oh boy, what a beautiful little head and enough hair for two."

Faith and Myles watched in the mirror, entranced as she delivered the head and began to turn the shoulders. All hands were on deck, ready with clamps, suction, a blanket.

"This is important, Mom and Dad. Myles, you keep hold of her hands. Nature's going to insist that she grab for her baby, and I have to keep a sterile field. Last push, Faith. Just don't push too hard. The baby's slippery, and I don't want to play catch."

The new parents were torn between staring into each other's eyes and watching the grand finale. With a grunt, Faith pushed, and they watched their baby enter the world together.

"A girl!" called Dr. Laurentz. "Congratulations, Mom and Dad, you have a beautiful baby girl!"

Her first cries filled the room with indignation. She was so beautiful and perfect. Faith began to cry and laugh with joy. Tears streamed down Myles's face, and he was laughing too.

"Our baby, our baby," they said, clinging together and raining kisses on each other.

"Please, let us hold our baby," she pleaded as soon as the umbilical cord was clamped and the placenta delivered.

"My pleasure," Dr. Laurentz said, beaming. "She looks perfect, obviously has healthy lungs, but in a little bit we need to check her over and get her weighed." She swaddled the baby in a blanket and handed the screaming bundle to Myles.

At his first touch the crying ceased. He cradled the

infant against his chest, then quickly placed her into Faith's outstretched arms. He joined them, one arm around his wife, the other wrapped around them both.

They kissed, nestling their child between them. A pair of dark bright eyes looked at them with such alertness, Faith couldn't believe she didn't really focus on her parents. A mop of wet hair framed the porcelain-doll face, and her little rosebud mouth quivered, though she remained quiet as they stroked her and proudly claimed her as theirs.

"Ten little fingers," Myles pronounced in a rough, emotional voice. "Ten little toes."

"And look at her nails! Have you ever seen anything so tiny and perfect?"

"Just you," he murmured. "I'm so proud of you both."

"We did it," Faith said, glowing. "We did it together."

The babe began to root against Faith's breast.

"Looks like you've got yourself a natural," a nurse observed. "All that work left your little girl hungry."

"I can nurse her?"

"I think that's what she's telling us she wants." Myles grinned broadly while he helped Faith shift aside the hospital gown to reveal a plumb breast. They watched, mesmerized, as the baby immediately began to seek a nipple.

Faith positioned her nipple next to the tiny mouth. "Oh!" she cried, amazed at how vigorously the infant sucked.

"Looks like we didn't get as ready as we thought." Myles chuckled while he coaxed a miniature fist to wrap round his little finger. "Our beautiful little girl," he crooned softly. "You're so smart, you already know how to hold Daddy's hand."

"Have you got a name picked out yet?" Dr. Laurentz asked.

Faith and Myles looked at each other. No words were needed to know that all the names they'd considered were wrong.

"Gloria," Faith whispered.

The tears brimming her eyes were mirrored in his.

"Gloria," he affirmed.

They kissed while Gloria hungrily drew nourishment. Her name was as perfect as herself, as fated as the joining of the hearts that loved her.

Thirteen

Faith yawned broadly while she gazed at the sleeping infant in her arms. If Dr. Laurentz's waiting room had had a bed, she would have gladly crawled into it. Gloria had begun to sleep through the night less than a week before, but Faith still hadn't caught up on her rest. Even though Myles was good about fetching the baby for two A.M. feedings, he couldn't supply the milk.

"You're lucky," the woman seated next to her said.

"I am," Faith readily agreed. Smiling in contentment, she asked, "Are you expecting?"

"I wish I could say so," the woman replied. "Unfortunately babies don't seem to be in my future."

"Oh, I'm sorry." Faith held Gloria closer, giving a silent prayer of thanks that she'd been blessed with the ability to conceive. "My sister couldn't have them either. I know what you must be going through."

"Well, all's not lost. We're hoping to find a surrogate if an adoption doesn't come through soon."

"A surrogate sounds like a good option." Faith smiled knowingly and stroked the soft curls framing Gloria's baby-doll face.

"We've been really let down a few times when an adoption didn't come through, so we're leaning more to the surrogate idea." The woman laughed and whispered confidentially, "My husband's already had a specimen frozen. He was terribly embarrassed."

"I guess it's pretty personal when it's your deposit." Faith chuckled.

"Oh, it wasn't the deposit he was so embarrassed about. It was having to produce one on the premises in a private room. He still turns red every time he remembers that experience. Not exactly one of the highlights of his life."

Faith's attention skidded into a wall of shock.

"'*On* the premises?'" she repeated in disbelief. "But I thought . . . maybe I didn't hear you right."

"Oh, yes," the other woman assured her. "Different cryobanks have different regulations. Some require a personal appearance, some don't. The one we used did. They have an excellent reputation."

"Which one did you use?" Faith asked urgently.

"I beg your pardon?" The woman looked at her strangely, apparently having come to the realization she'd somehow struck a nerve.

"Which one?" Faith was shaking, and Gloria began to fuss, setting her nerves and horrible suspicions on a wracking edge.

Staring at her in confusion the woman gave her the cryobank's name and address.

"Faith," Diane announced. "Your turn. And I'm just itching to hold that bundle of joy."

Faith managed to mutter her thanks to the other patient before moving jerkily in Diane's direction. She somehow got through the exam in a numb, zombie state as Dr. Laurentz asked routine questions and examined her.

"You've healed wonderfully and you're already close to your initial weight," Dr. Laurentz announced. "But are you feeling well? You don't seem yourself today."

"I'm . . . fine," Faith assured her even as her thoughts darted in all directions, looking for possible answers to the question swirling in her mind—and finding none. She had to get home quickly. She had to call the doctor in Denver and pray to God she was wrong. "Just . . . tired. Nothing some rest won't cure." Or desperately needed reassurance that her imagination was simply working overtime.

"In that case go home and enjoy your baby and husband." Dr. Laurentz chuckled. "Myles was about the proudest daddy I've ever seen. Every time I remember him racing up and down the hospital corridors and handing out cigars to strangers or the way he announced to anyone who'd listen that that was *his* baby at the nursery window, I start to laugh. Oh, and by the way, the nurses at the hospital really appreciated the candy and flowers he sent to them. So did Diane and I. He's a very special man, your husband."

"Yes," Faith agreed absent-mindedly. "Very special."

"You have the green light to resume your intimate relations. Just remember, you could already be fertile again, even if you're nursing. I always caution my patients to use birth control, unless they want another baby right away."

She and Myles had been counting the days until they heard those words. But now they barely registered, she was too distressed.

Miraculously she made it home without having an accident. Gloria's fussing had turned into screams of demand. While her mind rushed ahead, Faith went through the motions of changing and feeding the infant, then putting her to sleep.

Faith went to the phone, picking up the receiver with shaking hands. She didn't want to know. She *had* to know.

The other end picked up, and she said in a stilted voice, "Yes, this is Faith Wellington. I need to speak to Dr. Adams, please . . . No, it's not an emergency, or yes, it is. What I mean is, I need some information. . . . All right, I'll hold."

When the nurse came on the line, she identified herself.

"We haven't heard from you in so long, Faith. How are you?"

"Fine. . . . The reason I'm calling is that a lot of things have happened and, well, my sister died."

"How terrible for you."

"Yes, but the way it worked out is—I'm now

married to the private donor. We're raising the baby. We named her after my sister."

There was an awkward pause before the nurse said, "Congratulations. I'm glad everything worked out."

Had it? Oh, God, she could hardly breathe as she mentally prepared herself to ask the single question the whole fabric of her life depended upon.

She had to sound casual. She had to be careful not to arouse suspicion, since the doctor's office thought that all had been aboveboard in the family decision to use IUI. She and Gloria hadn't just duped Myles, they had misled the doctor too. He was reputable. If he'd known the truth, he would never have performed the procedure.

But had she, Faith, been duped as well?

"It did," she said, rushing on to add, "It worked out so well that we want everyone to know about our baby. I was just finishing birth announcements and realized I hadn't sent one to the cryobank. Could you give me their name and address?"

"Doesn't your husband have that information?"

"Of course!" She was beginning to hyperventilate and concentrated hard on getting some air into her lungs. "It's just that . . . he's out of town. On business. Out of the country. He might not be able to call until late tomorrow. I know it's an imposition, but I really wanted to finish this up today."

Dear Lord, please. Please just let them buy the half-baked excuse that sounded too flimsy even to her own ears.

"That's very considerate of you, wanting to thank them. I'll get the information off your chart. But just remember, this means I'll expect an announcement too," the nurse added with a laugh.

Faith waited a few minutes that seemed an eternity.

"Here you go, Faith. The name and address is . . ."

Faith closed her eyes and almost sank to the floor as the nurse gave her the information. She summoned a faint "thank you" and hung up, staring sightlessly at the receiver.

"Why?" she whispered. "*Why?*" she demanded. The last fragments of her hope surfaced, and she wondered if maybe the woman at Dr. Laurentz's was wrong. She had to be. Her sister couldn't have done something so twisted and cruel.

Fumbling with the phone book, Faith frantically got the necessary number and dialed the cryobank, which wasn't far from where she stood now. Stood as the ground seemed to open up, forcing her to stare into a big, black hole of nightmarish possibilities.

A receptionist answered. "May I help you?"

"Yes! I need to know if you take specimens collected off the premises? We're thinking of . . . my husband's shy and wants to make sure I can just bring it in."

"I'm sorry, but our policy dictates that all specimens must be collected in our office. We're very strict about that. It's for the security of our clients."

"Even for private donors?" She was grasping at anything to make the bottomless pit go away.

"That's right. Even for private donors. You can tell your husband the rooms are very private. All we need are some identification and his signature, and he can be on his way while we freeze it. We do it immediately, since sperm loses its potency about an hour or so after it's produced."

"But he can't—surely, you make some exceptions!"

"No. But if he's that upset about coming here, there is another cryobank not too far away. They're good and will accept specimens for private use over-the-counter. The only problem is the drive might take longer than—"

Faith hung up. She couldn't believe it. She'd conceived with a specimen from a cryobank that insisted on the donor's appearance. Only, Myles had never been there. He hadn't even known his sperm had been frozen until he'd stumbled on Gloria's papers.

Her mind and heart tried to reject the obvious. If Myles hadn't been there, it wasn't possible for them to freeze his seed. It had to come from . . . *who*? Who had gone there and impersonated Myles? And why? What man could have been close enough to Gloria to do such a thing for her? Not Martin. Whatever demons had driven her to deceive even her sister could never extend to risking the child's health with the consequences first cousins could spawn.

She had no answers, but the facts were glaringly real. She'd been inseminated with another man's donation. The child she'd carried and lovingly embraced with Myles as theirs couldn't be his. It was the only logical conclusion.

"Why did you do this to me?" she shrieked. "How could you, Gloria?"

Faith buried her face in her hands. Whatever answers she craved had gone to the grave with her sister. Had Gloria thought it would make no difference who the father was since Faith had vowed to let her adopt the child as her own? But if Gloria had thought that, why would she have said it was Myles's baby and confessed that she'd deceived him and risked losing his trust?

Faith was vaguely aware their baby was crying in the next room. *Their* baby? Her baby, not his.

She forced herself to go to the nursery. Her body was numb, as numb as her heart. She had to be numb to survive this terrible ordeal.

She moved mechanically, like an animated mannequin, until she reached the crying infant. Staring down into the crib, she felt her heart shattering the fragile, insulating shield of ice.

"Gloria," she sobbed. "Gloria." She held the baby to her, rocking back and forth as she sought to soothe herself more than the infant. Feeling her legs begin to give way, she stumbled to the white wicker rocker and held on to Gloria as if she were the only solid thing left in her shattered world.

The baby nursed hungrily, and Faith was grateful for the bond. She needed it now more than ever while she vainly tried to sift through each conversation with her sister that could hint at a clue.

Nothing.

Suddenly Faith quit rocking. In her mind a light shined brightly, accusingly, on the memory of Myles's near discovery of her sculpture.

Was it possible that Gloria had discovered the bust Faith had sculpted in loving tribute? Had Gloria guessed that they were in love with the same man? And if so, had she been desperate enough to have a child that she had led Faith to believe it was Myles's? Had she known it would be the ace, the one drawing card that Faith couldn't resist?

The air rushed from her lungs in a painful whoosh. Nothing else could explain it. And wasn't it true? Her sacrifice had been no sacrifice, no noble gesture or last-ditch effort to please her sister. She had agreed because it was Myles's baby; if it had been any other man's, she doubted that her nobility would have extended so far.

The tears began to roll down her cheeks while silent sobs wracked her chest. Her selfless decision had been more selfish than she had dared admit to herself until now. How desperate she must have been to have some part of him, as desperate as Gloria in another way. In spite of their sisterly devotion, the depth of their love, they had cheated each other.

That realization was almost as painful as knowing she had no choice but to confess the truth to Myles. All of it. Since the day he'd bared his soul, he had lived with the illusion they had no secrets. How would he take it? Would he love her just as much once he knew the baby wasn't his?

His words came rushing back to her: *"Even as I*

aged and could understand a man's resentment for having to raise a child that possibly belonged to some nameless stranger, there was always this . . . distance."

She couldn't bear his distance. If she'd needed him before they married, he had now become as essential as breathing to her existence.

"Faith? Faith, are you here?" Myles called from somewhere in the house.

Her head snapped up from her chest. How long had she been in here crying and mourning while Gloria peacefully slept in her arms?"

He stopped at the doorway, and the hall lighting cast his silhouette in a long black shadow on the nursery floor.

"Faith?" he repeated. "Is that you?"

"Yes," she whispered hoarsely.

"Why didn't you answer me? I was worried."

"I . . . Gloria's asleep."

"But why was the house dark? I tried calling to let you know I'd be home late, but no one answered."

"I guess . . . I didn't hear the phone ring."

She had to tell him. She couldn't. How could she ever push the horrid words past her lips?

The nursery light suddenly switched on. Fearfully she looked at Myles.

"Oh my God," he exclaimed as he gazed at her tear-streaked face. "What's wrong? What happened? Did the doctor find something bad?" he demanded as he closed the short distance between them.

When she only looked at him, shaking her head, he took Gloria from her and laid the baby gently in bed.

"Talk to me," he commanded. "Please, just talk to me. Tell me what's wrong."

"Myles," she sobbed, falling into his open arms. "Oh, Myles. It's terrible. You don't want to know. You don't want—"

"I want the truth. Just start talking and don't stop until you're through."

She collapsed against him, and he picked her up. Sitting in her rocker, he held her head against his chest and whispered his love against her hair.

Haltingly, she told him about her discovery, the words catching between dry sobs. "Our baby can't be yours. Please, tell me you don't hate me. Don't tell me you don't want us anymore or that you'll resent us every time you remember this."

Looking up at his face, she saw his shock. He tried to speak, but no words came. Then he lifted her up and carried her over to the baby's bed. She could feel the trembling of his large frame.

"I can't believe it," he finally whispered in a shaking voice. "I can't believe she's not mine. Because she is, Faith, and so are you. No matter what happened, you're both mine. But what tears me up even more than this hideous joke on the two of us is that you could actually believe I would love you any less or wish you out of my life. How could you have such little faith in me and the commitment I made when we took our vows?"

"I'm sorry, Myles. It's just that I love you so

much, it would kill me to lose you. And then I kept remembering what you'd said about your father."

His expression hardened, and he said roughly, "That has nothing to do with us or our family. We were made for each other, and you'd better never forget that again."

She had no answer but her own cry of relief, of gratitude to God that Myles did love her without condition, that his love had never been contingent on her giving him his own baby. He *did* love her, just for herself. Hadn't he told her so before? But then she'd never been able to fully believe it, had she?

"Do you have any idea why Gloria would have done such a thing?" he asked as he leaned over the crib and studied the baby's sleeping face with such love and tenderness it made her ache.

"I . . . I think I might have an answer. But it would be easier if I showed you something first. Something I should have shown you a long time ago." But she hadn't, and now she knew why. Without realizing it, she had waited for a signal, a sign that the depth of his love matched hers.

"I want a promise from you first," he said. "We promise to each other our baby will never know about this. We'll go to our graves with this secret binding us as tightly as the marriage vows we took."

He slid her down his length, and they embraced, sealing their pact within a fierce kiss. Myles tucked the blanket around their baby before she led him down the hall and into the studio. Faith stopped at the last sealed box that held her secret.

"Open it," she said. "Open it and look inside."

Impatiently he tore the box open and lifted the heavy mound inside. It was still wrapped. Faith could feel herself shaking again, not with fear but with anticipation.

He removed the layers of packaging, slowly unveiling the moment of truth. When it was done, he simply stared, disbelief and confusion etched into his features.

"This is me," he finally said. "Why do you have a sculpture of me? And why didn't you want me to see it?"

"Don't you know, Myles? Didn't you ever guess? I sculpted this before your wedding to Gloria."

His gaze met hers, comprehension slowly dawning, before his eyes turned once more to the plaster bust.

"You said he was married, the mystery man you loved who was the reason you moved away. He was—"

"How could you think it was anyone else?" she whispered brokenly as she caressed the sculpture. "It had to be you."

Fourteen

She waited, holding her breath.

"You loved me," he murmured. "Even then you loved me."

"I tried not to. I knew it was wrong because you belonged to someone else. But I learned that hearts have a way of making their own decisions. I didn't want to love you, but I did. And I do."

"What did I ever do to deserve so much?" He placed the sculpture on her table. "No man has a right to all I've been given."

Myles took her into his arms, his hands threading through her hair, tilting her head back.

"I kept it covered except when I needed you. You were never meant to see it. Until now."

He shook his head. "You don't know how this makes me feel."

"Tell me," she urged, pressing as close as she could get. "Show me."

His lips claimed hers urgently, fierce with demand.

"This is what you make me feel. It isn't gentle or patient, but it's deep and intense and so full it can make my heart ache."

"Then let me take the ache away." She slid her hand between them and curled her fingers over his groin. "Let me show you what you make me feel. Tonight it's reckless and desperate. I'm a woman who's craving to be consumed by her man."

He strained against her while a growl rumbled up from his soul. Somehow they made their way to their bed. Then his hands were on her, and quickly they stripped the clothes off each other.

With no baby between them, they fit hip-to-hip, hardness to softness, their bodies separated by only the thin sheath of protection.

"Give me the man inside you," she whispered. "Untamed, uninhibited, wild."

"You've asked for the beast and you've got him. The unwanted bastard stripped of the veneer he's spent a lifetime making others see. Aren't you afraid of him?"

"No. He pleases me. Excites me."

"But he's unpolished, not pretty or smooth."

"He's beautiful. Perfect for his woman."

"Then take me. Take the man who needs you more than he's ever needed you before."

"I need," she whimpered. "I need too."

He let her set the pace, and she knew she wouldn't be content with a gentle joining.

Finally their hoarse shouts of raw ecstasy resounded against the walls.

In the aftermath they stroked each other's faces,

kissed with tender lips. They joined hands and rocked together murmuring over and over "I love you . . . I love you . . . I love . . ."

"Myles," she said against his chest in a sleepy voice, "the phone."

"Ignore it," he muttered, clamping a leg over hers and managing to tangle the bedsheets tightly around them. "We already agreed it's just the three of us today. We don't need any visitors infringing on our time. They can call back tomorrow."

"It could be important."

"Ah, hell," he grumbled. "All right. But after this I'm unplugging the damn thing." He snatched up the phone and barked, "This is Wellington. . . . Oh, hello, Martin. Welcome back. You just interrupted some important negotiations, so I hope this is good."

Myles suddenly sat upright in bed, practically tumbling Faith onto the floor. He caught her and immediately tucked her under the haven of his arm. She played with the hair on his chest, feeling the glow of memories from the night before. Their exhausting romp had given way to hours of shared affection and strokes of loving tenderness.

"Okay . . . okay. Thanks for calling. We'll see you in another hour."

"What is it?" she asked, more than a little curious about what had prompted her husband's about-face. Myles shook his head, his expression disturbed.

"Martin's bringing over that certain something we've been joking about for months."

"Did he tell you what it is?"

"He did. And Faith, it's far from a joke."

"What is it?" She sat up too, anxiously clutching the sheets.

"A letter," he said, a frown creasing his brow. "It's from Gloria. She addressed it to us, in the event we ever married."

Faith rubbed her arms to ward the chill off her skin. She looked from Martin, who was holding Gloria and making an utterly lovable fool of himself, to Myles seated beside her and carefully fingering the sealed envelope. He looked at her in question, and she nodded.

"Read it, Myles," she whispered. He broke the seal and unfolded a crisp sheet of paper. The handwriting was weak but undeniably Gloria's.

He began to read aloud:

Dear Faith and Myles,

Since you are reading this, my wishes for you both have come true. You have found each other and married, as I know you were meant to. I must confess that in my hope to bring your destinies together, I lied to the two people I love most.

Myles, you must have found the papers I planted! Hopefully it didn't take you long, since Faith needs you while she carries your baby. But she needed you long before that.

Yes, Faith, I know. I know how much you love him and how you sacrificed your own feelings so that I could realize mine. The sculpture gave you away. I saw it years ago, but even before then any woman could have seen how deeply you felt, how much you cared for him. I could never blame you for loving him, Faith, especially knowing it had to be the reason you moved away and gave up everything you ever had or wanted out of love for me.

Such selfless sisterly love deserves an equal measure. So maybe you can forgive me for telling you that if only I had a baby to live for, I'd find the strength to make it through. But the doctor had already broken the news that I was terminal, and in my heart I knew it was true.

What I did wasn't very honest, but my intentions were good, and with my days numbered I was compelled to take the risk. If I didn't do something, you'd never tell Myles that you love him, and since he's as hardheaded as you, he wouldn't give himself the chance to find out that he could return your feelings because of his sense of loyalty to me. *Unless* you were carrying his baby. Ah, my grand scheme, it apparently worked! But then again, if I had thought it wouldn't, I never would have put you through this.

Kiss your baby for me each and every day, and please, when he or she is old enough, tell your child about Aunt Gloria. And Martin, give him my deepest affection and gratitude for the integral role he took on to let me play Cupid. I couldn't have done it without him.

Forgive me for any pain my deceptions may have caused along the way, because I've never loved anyone in the world half as much as you, my dear ones, my friends. Now you must love each other with all the fire that shines so brightly from your souls. You've warmed me with it and for that, I thank you. It is my dying wish that you spend the rest of your lives being happy, living fully. Remember me, but never with sadness. I don't want your guilt or your tears. Only your smiles and memories of shared love and affection that even the grave can never steal.

All my love, eternally—
Gloria

"She knew," Faith said, swiping at her flowing tears. "All these years she knew."

"Gloria always saw what other people didn't."

"I'm afraid I never gave Gloria credit for being so wily," Faith admitted with a small laugh.

"She got us both," Myles agreed. "We were lucky to have had her in our lives. And lucky us to have each other."

"And Gloria," Faith reminded him, nodding at the cooing infant.

Myles looked at Martin with a puzzled frown. "But what about the cryobank? Gloria said the baby was ours."

They both looked at Martin, who had stopped in mid "goochey-goochey-goo."

"Of course the baby's yours," he said, clearing his throat awkwardly. "Why wouldn't you think it's yours?"

Faith and Myles explained the crucial facts surrounding Faith's discovery.

"Oh, cripes," Martin groaned. "I can't believe you found that out." He rolled his eyes heavenward and groaned again. "Gloria, you owe me big for this."

Getting up, he handed the baby to his father. "Okay, Myles, *you're* the father, got that? Faith is the mother. I never dreamed I'd have to tell anyone this, and I made Gloria promise she wouldn't breathe a word, not even to Faith." Thrusting a hand into his hair, he began to pace.

"Here's what happened. You both know Gloria and I were—*are*—this close." He held up two crossed fingers. "Lord knows why, because two people were never more different. Anyway, I could never refuse Gloria anything, especially when it meant the world to her."

Martin slid a finger beneath his collar as though it were suddenly too tight. "There were two cryobanks she could possibly go to. Since time was of the essence, the perfect one that didn't require, uh, personal deposits, was too far away. There was only one way she could have a specimen frozen in time, and that was to use the clinic closest to your house."

Turning a very bright red, Martin rushed on quickly. "She gave me Myles's specimen, along with some credit cards and his Social Security card. I went to the lab, disappeared into a room, waited five minutes, and went to the counter to hand over the specimen Gloria gave me. I told them my license was lost, and since it was for personal purposes, they accepted the ID I had and didn't question the forged signature.

"They promised to freeze it immediately, and I got the hell out before my rising blood pressure put me in a coma. It was the most humiliating experience of my life, by far the most unethical act I've ever committed. It could have jeopardized my career. I wouldn't have done it for anyone but Gloria, and as wrong as it was, I'd do it again. My only regret is that the two of you found out."

"Then . . ." Faith looked excitedly from Martin to Gloria to Myles. "She's *ours*? *Really . . . ours*?"

"The real McCoy. The genuine article. I just played delivery boy."

Faith bounded off the couch and threw her arms around her cousin's neck. Kissing him several times on both cheeks, she whispered, "Thank you, thank you. Oh, Lord, thank you . . ."

"Hmmm," Martin mused, "If I'd known I might get this kind of reception, I would have come clean a lot sooner."

They bid him good-bye soon after, with grins as wide as Texas.

"She's *ours*." Faith laid her head against her husband's chest while she cradled the sleeping babe in her arms. Myles cupped her face in both hands and tilted it up until she looked into the piercing depths of his eyes.

"She was always ours," he vowed. "She's sleeping." He nodded at the baby before his lips pursed suggestively and he tilted his head in the direction of the stairs.

"Soundly, I hope," Faith said as they moved eagerly toward their destination.

Gazing heavenward, she couldn't help but think how fitting it was that a new life nestled close to her breast while another smiled blessings from above.

Blessings and miracles. Gloria slept peacefully as they laid her down and proceeded to their room.

There they poured out their love, then lay replete in each other's arms. Whispering, cuddling, loving. A man and a woman making their own miracle . . . behind closed doors.

THE EDITOR'S CORNER

Come join the celebration next month as LOVESWEPT reaches an important milestone—the publication of LOVESWEPT #500! The journey has been exceptionally rewarding, and we're proud of each book we've brought you along the way. Our commitment to put the LOVESWEPT imprint only on the best romances is unwavering, and we invite you to share with us the trip to LOVESWEPT #1000. One step toward that goal is the lineup of six fabulous reading treasures we have in store for you.

Please give a rousing welcome to Linda Jenkins and her first LOVESWEPT, **TOO FAR TO FALL**, #498. Linda already has five published romances to her credit, and you'll soon see why we're absolutely thrilled to have her. **TOO FAR TO FALL** features one rugged hunk of a hero, but Trent Farraday is just too gorgeous for Miranda Hart's own good. His sexy grin makes her tingle to her toes when he appears at her door to fix a clogged drain. How can a woman who's driven to succeed be tempted by a rogue who believes in taking his time? With outrageous tenderness, Trent breaches Miranda's defenses and makes her taste the fire in his embrace. Don't miss this wonderful romance by one of our New Faces of '91!

In **THE LADY IN RED**, LOVESWEPT #499, Fayrene Preston proves why that color has always symbolized love and passion. Reporter Cassidy Stuart is clad in a slinky red-sequined sheath when she invades Zach Bennett's sanctuary, and the intriguing package ignites his desire. Only his addictive kisses make Cassidy confess that she's investigating the story about his immensely successful toy company being under attack. Zach welcomes the lovely sleuth into his office and as they try to uncover who's determined to betray him, he sets out on a thrilling seduction of Cassidy's guarded heart. As always, Fayrene Preston writes with spellbinding sensuality, and the wonderful combination of mystery and romance makes this book a keeper.

Glenna McReynolds sets the stage for an enchanting and poignant tale with **MOONLIGHT AND SHADOWS**, LOVESWEPT #500. Jack Hudson blames the harvest moon for driving him crazy enough to draw Lila Singer into his arms the night they meet and to kiss her breathless! He has no idea the beautiful young widow has relinquished her dreams of love. Lila knows there could only be this sensual heat between them—they have nothing else in common. Jack has never backed down from a challenge, and convincing Lila to take a chance on more than one special night together is the sweetest dare of all. A beautiful love story that you won't be able to put down.

Guaranteed to heat your blood is **THE SECRET LIFE OF ELIZABETH McCADE**, LOVESWEPT #501 by Peggy Webb. Black Hawk burns with the same restless fever that Elizabeth McCade keeps a secret, and when this legendary Chickasaw leader hides from his enemies in her house, he bewitches her senses and makes her promise to keep him safe. But nothing can protect her from the uncontrollable desire that flares between them. Elizabeth is haunted by painful memories, while Hawk has his own dark shadows to face, and both must overcome fears before they can surrender to ecstasy. Together these two create a blazing inferno of passion that could melt the polar ice caps!

Marvelous talent Laura Taylor joins our fold with the sensational **STARFIRE**, LOVESWEPT #502. With his irresistible looks, business superstar Jake Stratton is every woman's fantasy, but professor Libby Kincaid doesn't want to be his liaison during his visiting lecturer series—even though his casual touch makes her ache with a hunger she can't name. Jake's intrigued by this vulnerable beauty who dresses in shapeless clothes and wears her silky hair in a tight bun. But Libby doesn't want to want any man, and capturing her may be the toughest maneuver of Jake's life. A real winner from another one of our fabulous New Faces of '91!

Finally, from the magical pen of Deborah Smith, we have **HEART OF THE DRAGON**, LOVESWEPT #503. Set in exotic Thailand, this fabulous love story features Kash Santelli—remember him from *The Silver Fox and the Red Hot Dove*? Kash is prepared to frighten Rebecca Brown off, believing she's a greedy schemer out to defraud her half sister, but once he meets her, nothing about the minister's daughter suggests deception. Indeed, her feisty spirit and alluring innocence make him want to possess her. When Rebecca finds herself in the middle of a feud, Kash must help—and Rebecca is stunned by her reckless desire for this powerful, enigmatic man. Riveting, captivating—everything you've come to expect from Deborah Smith . . . and more.

And (as if this weren't enough!) be sure to look for the four spectacular novels coming your way from FANFARE, where you'll find only the best in women's fiction. **REAP THE WIND** by bestselling author Iris Johansen is the thrilling conclusion to the unforgettable Wind Dancer trilogy. **THE SWANSEA DES-TINY** by much-loved Fayrene Preston is the long-awaited prequel to her SwanSea series from LOVESWEPT. Critically acclaimed Virginia Lynn delivers another humorous and exciting Wild West historical in **CUTTER'S WOMAN**, and Pamela Morsi follows the success of her first book with **COURTING MISS HATTIE**, a very touching story of a spinster who finds true love.

What a terrific month of reading in store for you from LOVESWEPT and FANFARE!

With warmest wishes,

Nita Taublib

Nita Taublib
Associate Publisher, LOVESWEPT
Publishing Associate, FANFARE
Bantam Books
666 Fifth Avenue
New York, NY 10103

FANFARE

Enter the marvelous new world of **Fanfare**!
From sweeping historicals set around the globe to
contemporary novels set in glamorous spots,
Fanfare means great reading.
Be sure to look for new **Fanfare** titles each month!

On Sale in August:
GENUINE LIES
By Nora Roberts
author of PUBLIC SECRETS
*In Hollywood, a lady learns fast: the bad can be beautiful,
and the truth can kill.*

FORBIDDEN
By Susan Johnson
author of SWEET LOVE, SURVIVE
*Daisy and the Duc flirt, fight, and ultimately flare up in
one of the hottest and most enthralling novels
Susan Johnson has ever written.*

BAD BILLY CULVER
By Judy Gill
author of SHARING SUNRISE
*A fabulous tale of sexual awakening, scandal, lies and a
love that can't be denied.*

**THE SYMBOL OF GREAT WOMEN'S
FICTION FROM BANTAM**
Ask for these books at your local bookstore.

AN 323 8/91

FANFARE

Enter the marvelous new world of **Fanfare**!
From sweeping historicals set around the globe to
contemporary novels set in glamorous spots,
Fanfare means great reading.
Be sure to look for new **Fanfare** titles each month!

On Sale in September:

REAP THE WIND
By Iris Johansen

*A dazzling contemporary novel of passion, revenge, and a search
for the famous Wind Dancer statue.*

THE SWANSEA DESTINY
by Fayrene Preston

*The long-awaited prequel to the "SwanSea Place" LOVESWEPT series.
Scorching passion -- enduring love -- in an era of
splendor and despair.*

CUTTER'S WOMAN
by Virginia Lynn, author of RIVER'S DREAM

*"Filled with strong characterizations and one adventure after
another, this book is a joy to read." -Rendezvous*

COURTING MISS HATTIE
by Pamela Morsi, author of HEAVEN SENT

*"This is a story that lives in your heart long after it is done. . . .
Excellent." --Rendezvous*

**THE SYMBOL OF GREAT WOMEN'S
FICTION FROM BANTAM**
Ask for these books at your local bookstore.

AN 333 - 9/91

If you loved **FOLLOW THE SUN**, don't miss
Deborah Smith's next book from FANFARE, on
sale in October:

*A man and a woman who couldn't have been
more different -- all it took to bring them
together was a...*

Miracle

by

Deborah Smith

An unforgettable story of love and the collision of
worlds. From a shanty in the Georgia hills to a televi-
sion studio in L.A., from a prestigious Atlanta hospital
to the heat and dust of Africa to glittering Paris nights
-- with warm, humorous, passionate characters,
MIRACLE weaves a spell in which love may be im-
probable but never impossible.

"This innovative author should not be missed . . . Ms.
Smith knows how to carry off a . . . love story that charms
your socks off." -- *Romantic Times*

"A splendid romance author, Deborah Smith's star just
keeps rising. Passion, humor, poignancy -- her novels
have it all." -- *Rendezvous*

**THE SYMBOL OF GREAT WOMEN'S
FICTION FROM BANTAM**

Ask for it at your favorite book store

AN322 8/91

"Ms. Gill taps into our deepest emotions in this provocative love story, proving herself skillfully adept at touching our hearts." — <u>Rave Reviews</u>

Bad Billy Culver

By Judy Gill

Betrayal . . . a dark secret . . . a love that would outlast slander and time and taboo. . .

Billy Culver grew up poor, handsome as the devil -- and twice as bad. Arlene Lambert grew up in a home full of the security and elegance old money could provide. And she loved the housekeeper's son. Suddenly, scorned and condemned for a transgression he did not commit, Billy was driven out of town.

Now, rich and powerful and determined, Bad Billy Culver is back -- and dead set on getting revenge. When he confronts Arlene, he is tormented by guilt . . . renewed feelings of desire . . . and echoes of love. Arlene has never stopped loving Billy. But it is a love she cannot act on -- because of a secret so profound, so shameful that she will lose love itself to keep it from coming to light.

"This is incredible reading. Both protagonists are so real you can touch them . . . . A definite must!" *--Rendezvous*

THE SYMBOL OF GREAT WOMEN'S FICTION FROM BANTAM
On sale now at your local bookstore.

AN 335 - 9/91